Mantis Prayers

by
Rich Polk

Copyright 2014 by Richard Polk

All rights reserved. No part of this book may be reproduced, stored in a retrieval system, or transmitted in any form or by any means without the prior written permission of the publishers, except by a reviewer who may quote brief passages in a review to be printed in a newspaper, magazine, or journal.

First Printing.

Excerpts of Emily Dickinson's poems used in this work are in the public domain.
Source: THE POEMS OF EMILY DICKINSON, edited by Thomas H. Johnson, Cambridge, Mass.: The Belknap Press of Harvard University Press, Copyright © 1951, 1955 by the President and Fellows of Harvard College. Copyright © renewed 1979, 1983 by the President and Fellows of Harvard College. Copyright © 1914, 1918, 1919, 1924, 1929, 1930, 1932, 1935, 1937, 1942, by Martha Dickinson Bianchi. Copyright © 1952, 1957, 1958, 1963, 1965, by Mary L. Hampson.

ISBN: 978-1502898425
CreateSpace Independent Publishing Platform
www.amazon.com

Printed in the United States of America

For Fred and his loving wife

A note on the First Edition

The author intended to begin each chapter of this novel with a few appropriate lines of Emily Dickinson's poetry. It was hoped that this would help connect the reader to the English professor protagonist of the story as well as give each chapter a predictive motif. To facilitate this, he requested permission to use these fifty-six snippets, each with a complete credit and citation, from Harvard University Press, the owner of the copyrights. Given the limited number of readers this book will probably attract, the author expected that receiving permission would be a mere formality. When the university requested a payment in excess of five hundred dollars, an alternative course of action was required.

He chose to leave the poetry references but delete the forty-six snippets where the copyrights still apply, leaving untouched the ten poems which are now in the public domain. The curious reader may wish to look up the referenced lines of verse and thus discover what the author—and Miss Dickinson—had in mind. It is hoped a reader so inclined will appreciate the reduction in the book's cover price before complaining of the additional effort involved. For those finding Harvard's behavior deplorable, the author suggests that it pales against the realization that the same university graduated arguably the least grounded scholar of United States constitutional law of all time. So armed, this graduate was unleashed to deploy his perverted ideas against the American people and accelerate the real-life version of this fictional account. *–Rich Polk*

Those who read the "Revelations"
Must not criticize
Those who read the same Edition –
With beclouded Eyes!

> Emily Dickinson, from No. 168

1

Russell closed the tattered volume of Emily Dickinson's poetry and shoved it back across his desk. Rolling his chair back, he looked again, perhaps for the twentieth time, at the brief case next to his feet. What had the world come to?

Glancing at his watch revealed that office hours had ended forty-five minutes ago. Not one of his students had come to seek his help. Again.

He retrieved the briefcase and opened it. He stuffed a few folders of student essays inside and then placed the book of verses in its place of honor at the top before latching the case closed.

His eyes were drawn out the window where a sunny fall day was drawing to an end. He had always loved autumn. At least he had back when life was sweeter and he was more connected to it. The glorious beauty of this day helped him remember. The colors of the leaves were at their peak, and the sun shining through them underscored this fact. No place was this more apparent than along the driveway that led from the Mansion to the lot where Russell routinely parked his car. The oaks and maples were massive, having been planted as good size saplings before the home had been finished, more than a century earlier. Today, the canopy created by these huge hardwoods was inviting to one and all. A long file of students streamed down the sidewalk toward their late afternoon classes held in the former home of a railroad tycoon. Russell stole a glance at his briefcase in response to seeing a university security officer drive his black and white patrol car in the opposite direction down the narrow drive. He shuddered slightly at this newly conditioned response. Reassured, he continued to look out the window noting that a small group of students had dropped their books and stepped out of their sandals to toss around a Frisbee on the lawn. It was, he concluded, an inviting scene. His invitation, however, had not arrived.

For twenty-six years Russell Grayson had loved his job as a tenured professor at Schuyler University. Teaching three sections of Freshman English as well as a 19th Century American Literature class had its challenges and rewards. But now his career was unfulfilling. He completed his instruction and maintained a vigil during office hours in rote, uninspired fashion. Out of habit, or perhaps desperation, he had turned to reading passages from his ragged copy of Dickinson poetry to find that inspiration. However, he was quickly distracted as his mind analyzed why no students would bother to seek him out for help. The students could see it. He was no longer the teacher he used to be. He was just going through the motions.

Each evening at this time he would admit to himself that he had shortchanged his students again. He would resolve to improve on the following day, to deliver a lecture worthy of their tuition dollars and compliant with his teaching contract. But the next day always proved no better than the one before. He would wake to remember his loss. How everything had changed. It was two months now. He was nearly helpless to change much of anything in his life.

And yet— Yesterday, he had taken action. He had done something so alien to his nature, so different from anything he had ever done before. The weight of that action pulled at his soul, burdening his mind even as it weighted his briefcase.

So now he stepped out the rear door of the building. The warmth of the mid-October afternoon was enough to make him regret wearing his tweed sport coat. However, because of the bulky brown leather briefcase he carried and the relentless flow of oncoming students, he had to leave his jacket on. He must not, would not, set the briefcase down—even for a second. Instead, with the case still held in one hand, he hiked his pants up. The thumbs of both hands grabbed his belt which hung loosely around his waist despite being racked in to the innermost belt hole. Walking on, he noticed again the tassel on his loafer that Rufus had nearly chewed off. He was having troubles with his loss, too.

Along the way, he gazed upward, towards the treetops. Squirrels scurried among the upper branches, stopping occasionally to harvest some acorns, often dropping a few in random bombing missions on the pedestrians below. A pair of jays squawked loudly as they flitted about, their attractive blue, black, and white feathers completely overpowered by the yellows, oranges, and golds of the background leaves. Even so, he felt like an uninvited intruder at this spectacle.

The waves of students through which he passed were unknown to him. These were the early arrivals of the "Continuing Education Division", commuters to evening classes at Schuyler University. His charges were diurnal denizens, who, at this hour, mostly had returned to their homes or dorm rooms. Or perhaps to a Frisbee game? No, he recognized none of the disc tossers.

He arrived at his car, a forest green Forester, which sat in the corner of the lot. His late arrival each morning resulted in him taking whatever was left in the faculty lot. Now, with most of his colleagues gone before him, and the smaller number of C.E.D. faculty having no interest in parking in remote corners, he found himself very much alone. He stepped into the car and placed his briefcase on the passenger seat. He looked about tentatively. Seeing no one near, he ignored his mind's own cautions. He opened the briefcase and plunged his hand through the English compositions until he found it, resting on the bottom.

It was warmer than he had expected. A mystery writer might have called it "cold steel," but what his hand wrapped around seemed to have a warmth of its own, although its metallic composition was not in doubt. Looking around again, he withdrew his hand and the Glock 9 mm pistol it held. The weapon had more heft than he remembered. When he first purchased it, yesterday, he had handled it a great deal. It hadn't weighed so much. Then he recalled that today it was loaded, the grip filled with ten rounds of semi-jacketed hollow point ammunition.

Purchasing the gun had been easier than he had imagined. He had borrowed a laptop computer from the storage room where Schuyler stored computers to be issued to students. Using a mock student's internet identity used for testing purposes, he had signed on to the wireless network and was soon exploring the dark recesses of cyberspace. He surfed through the black market sites, an area of electronic commerce that had grown exponentially in recent years in response to the faltering economy. Soon he was at a website that boasted of its ability to sell just about anything to just about anybody. It wasn't long until he had joined a conversation with "Malcolm Y." Within hours he met Malcolm in a parking lot in Passaic. Cash was exchanged for unregistered weapon and illegal ammunition, a slight nod by each man sealed the deal, and the two parties drove away in opposite directions.

Russell took another look around. Still no one nearby. His secret was safe.

He pulled back the slide and released it, chambering a round. Very smooth. This was a precision machine. And now it was ready. Ready to kill. The unanswered question: was he ready?

He took yet another look around the parking lot. He was still alone. He then carefully unloaded the gun and returned the round to the magazine, and thrust the magazine back into the grip. He replaced the weapon in his briefcase, once again near the bottom. He closed the case, started his car, and headed home.

Even before he reached the campus gate Russell was overcome by the feeling of loneliness which had become such a prominent part of his life over the past two months. As an antidote, he switched on the car radio, although it had always proved inadequate in the past. The news stories that greeted him lacked novelty or freshness. Instead, they were laden with a feeling of chronic malaise and an unwavering oppressive tone.

"…thousands of refugees. Israeli tanks continued to barrage Eilat for the third consecutive day since the city was captured by Egyptian forces. Israeli jets also struck several targets along the border between Israel and Egypt.

"Meanwhile, in the Golan Heights, United States F-15 fighters flew thirteen sorties against Syrian strongholds along the border with Israel. President Benson, speaking to reporters, again insisted that the U.S. involvement would continue to be limited to tactical air support to our long-time ally who is being attacked on two fronts."

Karen was there, Russell was sure of it. He had had misgivings—the way any parent would—when his daughter enlisted in the Air Force after the terrorist attack on Houston. But there was no stopping her. She got her determination from her mother, and Meredith's consent effectively silenced any protest he might make. He had his own misgivings about his reaction to 9/11. He had been quick to use a young daughter as a valid excuse to continue his graduate studies and to let other volunteers fight in Afghanistan and Iraq.

Karen wouldn't divulge her location, of course. She had too much discipline for that—the same discipline that she had exhibited at the academy and in flight school. But her emails had become increasingly terse lately, lacking the description of little anecdotes that a state-side deployment possessed. And the posting times now were odd, but consistent with a seven hour time difference.

It was ironic, of course, that the battlefield would be the Golan Heights. He remembered looking at Meredith with disbelief when she had proposed they spend part of their summer vacation on a kibbutz in Israel.

"I think it would add a new dimension to my teaching of economics," she had said.

"You—the free market economist—on a kibbutz for two weeks?"

"Yes! It should give me a fresh perspective!"

"But in the Golan Heights?" Russell had countered. "Right in the cross-hairs of every anti-Israeli government or crackpot who insists Israel shouldn't even exist? You couldn't find a kibbutz in the Galilee?"

"My contact has connections in the Golan. Volunteers are hard to come by."

"Exactly my point!"

"Aw, come on! That adds to the excitement!"

And so it was decided. As with nearly everything, Russell had difficulty saying "no" to his wife. She had saved him the ignominy of a vocal "told you so" after the weeks of working with their backs had brought them closer together. It had been near the end of their stay that Karen had been conceived.

Russell was jarred from his reflective mood

by the continuing news broadcast.

"In Washington, Republican and Liberty Tree Party leaders again called on President Benson to schedule presidential elections. Speaking from the Rose Garden, the president answered his critics.

"'I, too, would like nothing better than to return to stable times and allow the American people to exercise once again their rights at the polls. However, until we are able to ensure free elections, without the threats of violent, anarchist forces, we must continue to operate under martial law for the protection of all the people. The murderers of John Landers are still at large. Until they are brought to justice, all future candidates will be forced to campaign under intimidating conditions, conditions that are contrary to the freedoms associated with a democratic electoral process of our great nation.'"

As usual, Russell found the president's voice annoying. He hated the way he chopped his sentences into little pieces, as if he were making it easier for a reporter to write them down. Or maybe the software magnate turned politician did not believe his audience was capable of understanding any phrase more than three words long. As for content, the leader of the free world treaded water more frequently than he swam deliberately in a specific direction.

"It was two months ago" the newscaster continued, "that John Landers, a Liberty Tree Party presidential hopeful, and four others were killed by a group of hooded gunmen while campaigning in Fort Wayne, Indiana. At the time, opinion polls placed Landers five percentage points ahead of President Benson."

Russell felt the rage ignite in his chest and then rush up his throat as he shouted at the radio. "She wasn't an 'other'! She had a name: Meredith Grayson! She had a heart! She had a mind! She had a soul!"

A ...
[Deleted]   ... *joy*

Emily Dickinson, from No. 1185 Lines 1-2

2

Pulling into his driveway, Russell shut off the Forester and sat back in the seat, expelling a large breath in celebration of surviving the drive home. Then, another sigh, in exasperation at the amount of work that had been postponed as revealed by a quick inspection of the property. The yard, a flat one hundred by two hundred foot plot, was in need of mowing. The grass was curling over onto itself, and where the crabgrass was gaining a foothold, its tall shafts, loaded with seeds, exceeded ankle height. The shrubbery around the house was thick and bushy, and here and there, nightshade vines and glossy poison ivy leaves proclaimed their unchallenged success at invading the beds and intertwining among their hosts. The mums, needing thinning again this year, were overcrowding their neighbors as the multitude of blossoms atop each plant provided the few colors of the setting, primarily whites and violets.

The house, a two-story colonial with a modest portico over the front door, was substantial enough, making itself at home with a dozen of its cousins on Arlington Drive. They all shared the same floor plan, though some were reversed, and each sported unique combinations of brick facades below, different colored siding above, and contrasting shutters throughout. All of this had been done to make each home appear different. But Russell was keenly aware that the siding on his house was different by its need for a coat of paint. Meredith had called his attention to it last spring. The brutal heat of the summer had led him to plead for postponement to the fall. That dreadful afternoon in August threatened to extend the delay indefinitely.

He grabbed his briefcase and stepped out of the car. He extended a short wave to Dieter, his German immigrant neighbor, who was tending his already fastidiously manicured property. Dieter returned the wave, but with, Russell thought, a bit of disdain. Funny, he thought, how sympathetic looks only a month ago had morphed into mild disapproval as Russell's neglect of his property was having an impact on the appearance of the neighborhood.

He did not dwell on such thoughts, however, as he ascended the steps to the porch and braced himself for the explosion of unrestrained joy he knew was to follow. His key in the lock initiated a series of whimpers from within, which increased in volume as the door was opened. As the gap neared a half-foot, the door knob was pulled from his hand as Rufus, a rust-tinged golden retriever with a fluorescent green tennis ball in his mouth, wedged himself through the opening. The dog sprang from the stoop and began describing large circles in the front yard at high speed.

Russell placed his case just inside the door, and returned to stand on the flagstone steps. Rufus seized this opportunity to sprinkle the trunk of a dogwood tree with a day's worth of liquid intake. He returned to his owner to offer him the tennis ball and receive Russell's greeting of brisk rubs to head, neck and ribs.

Russell tossed the ball into the air, and Rufus twisted and twirled below it before jumping into the air to make a clean catch. Once he returned to earth, Rufus resumed his elliptical orbit, spurred on by Russell's clapping hands. The pair repeated this pattern of play several times before Rufus, his tongue wagging in counterpoint to his tail at the opposite end, resigned to his fatigue, and led his owner into the house.

It was always the smell of the house that struck him. He didn't smell anything in particular, nor did he miss a particular aroma that he had remembered from the past. Something was different, though, and he was certain of it despite his inability to catalog it. Perhaps it was the absence of cooking odors. Since she died, he hardly ate, and rarely cooked. He was barely able to muster enough enthusiasm to boil some pasta or microwave a pre-packaged dinner. Perhaps it was Rufus. Bending over the dog to deliver a rub behind the ears, he took a whiff. The dog could use a bath—yet another victim of his neglect. Was it her perfume? Or maybe her natural scent, of which he may only have been aware subliminally? He wasn't sure. But it wasn't the same. Nothing was the same.

Russell moved down the central hall towards the family room and kitchen, carrying his briefcase with him. He was uncomfortable if it was not within his sight. He set it down on the floor and collapsed into the reclining chair, slumped into the upholstery, and closed his eyes. Almost immediately, he felt Rufus's chin on his thigh and opened his eyes to gaze at the canine's large brown ones. Unconsciously, he began to stroke the animal's fur while searching its eyes for some glint of understanding. He knew there could be none. Only recently had Rufus stopped wandering from room to room, obviously searching for Meredith. The dog could offer no answers, only a reassuring presence, a fragile link to what once was. As if sensing his owner's sadness, Rufus placed a paw on Russell's leg and began to nudge him.

"You're right, boy. No use feeling sorry for myself. Whadaya say we grade some essays?"

Rufus stepped back and began to wag his tail

energetically, letting out a short bark.

"Yes, yes, I dare say my young scholars will be anxious to learn their grades."

Russell first extracted the Dickinson collection and set it aside, then reached into his case and grabbed the majority of the papers he had haphazardly dropped into it before leaving his office. On the second dip, he felt the handgun, and withdrew it to inspect it once again. Rufus cocked his head at an angle.

"You are quite right, sport. What am I doing with this? Has our world really changed that much?"

Russell turned the weapon to inspect it from several angles. Rufus yawned, his pink tongue curling into his mouth.

"Bored, are you, Rufus? Really? In these exciting times?"

The dog cocked his head again, and wagged his tail.

Russell sighed and walked to the pantry. He retrieved a bag of kibble, and then grabbed a half-used can of dog food from the refrigerator. Removing the plastic cap, he mixed the canned food with some of the dry dog food, all under the watchful eye of Rufus.

"You are fortunate, my friend, to be a carefree animal. You don't know about the shortages—about the empty shelves in the stores. You haven't complained that I've been mixing more dry food into your meals? Of course not! You are content!"

Russell placed the food on the floor and stepped back as the dog attacked it.

"Ah, but if you were smarter, you wouldn't be content. The thousands of government programs, why, that's only justification to create more! And you wouldn't be content until you got *your share*. You'd be jealous if your neighbor earned more than you. And you won't be content, in fact, you'll show your contempt, as long as the 'rich' sit high and mighty."

He continued to watch the dog, who slid the stainless bowl across the floor. When he had finished, Rufus stood, shifting his weight from one foot to the other.

"That's it! Get agitated! Get involved—but not too much. Be pragmatic. Be prudent. Put a 'Benson for President' sign in your front yard even as you quietly support the Liberty Tree Party. Maybe that will spare you from the damage the hooligans inflict on their political opponents."

Rufus growled softly, the growl erupting as a bark.

"Shhh! I thought you were content! Content is the way to be if you disagree with our rulers. Because if you defy this political machine…"

Russell dropped to one knee, as if helpless against the oppression he had described. Rufus stepped forward and rested his chin on Russell's thigh.

"Meredith wasn't content. She wrote some treatises, published some articles. She was to be Chief Economic Advisor to John Landers…and look what happened to her."

Russell looked again at the Glock, lying on the counter. "'God created men. Colt made them equal.' A 'six-shooter' won the West. I'm not sure a semi-automatic holding ten rounds will be enough today."

Russell rose and returned the firearm to his case and removed the remainder of the essays. After a little more searching, he withdrew a red pen and set to grading the papers.

"And I, my dear Rufus, shall be content. Content to teach these young freshmen clarity, organization, development, grammar, and punctuation in the hopes that should they graduate and somehow obtain a job, they'll be able to write somewhat coherently."

I ... –
   [Deleted]   away –

Emily Dickinson, from No.739 Lines 1-2

3

They kept coming, every one unique, yet monotonous in their ceaseless flow. Car after car after bus after truck, eight lanes of traffic doubling for the tolls, then constricting to four to cross the upper deck of the bridge.

From his perch, thirty feet up in the bridge's west tower, Paul Robinson could see the traffic, moving like a hot lava flow through the gap in the Palisades, between the office buildings, under the toll booth superstructure, and towards his post on the George Washington Bridge. He wouldn't have thought his desert camouflage uniform would be effective in this urban setting. However, the gray bridge towers, the lifeless gray sky, and the gray mist that hovered just above the bridge and screened the skyscrapers in the distance to his left made for a nondescript background where it was easy to blend in. He wondered how many of the drivers below him were even aware that he was there, watching them.

Watching for what, he could not really say. Terrorists, of course. A vigil had been kept here for terrorists since 2001. The events in Houston—the poisoning of the water supply that had led to the slow, painful deaths of so many thousands of souls—had heightened the alert, naturally. But what constituted suspicious behavior, much less terrorist threatening behavior, if the people stayed in their vehicles and just kept driving? That woman there: steering with the heels of her hands, a coffee cup in her right, a cellular phone in her left. Was she suspicious? Or how about that guy in a suit, his right index finger working away at extracting a mother lode of nasal congestion from his sinuses. That black guy, his body gyrating to the amplified rhythm of some equatorial drum beat—him maybe? Or maybe that guy in the BMW who looks like he's half-asleep? Isn't it always the quiet ones you have to watch?

Now there was a new threat: anarchists. Or from whomever it was that martial law was supposed to be protecting the public. They were no easier to spot than the terrorists—less so, in fact, if you believed Jasper, who was convinced that the "towelheads" should have been singled out for special anti-terrorist scrutiny. The murder of John Landers had precipitated the declaration of martial law, and with it, increased security at post-9/11 high risk venues and new locations, as well.

Paul re-checked the safety on his M16 for the fourth time since climbing up to his post. There was no way he would allow an accidental discharge of his weapon to injure anyone. In fact, if he didn't have to carry a firearm it would be just as well for him. He remembered his Uncle Ken's reaction when he had told him he had joined the National Guard. Ken, always so convivial with a smile on his face and a joke on his lips, had turned sullen, his eyes all but disappearing beneath overhanging eyebrows. "I don't think it's a good idea, Paulie," he had said. "The Guard's nothing but a bunch of high strung weekend warriors—over-armed and under-trained. It's too easy for you to get hurt or for you to hurt someone."

"I want to be there to help," Paul had answered, "like last year, after the hurricane. I saw what a difference they made in our town. I want to help like that."

"Maybe you will," the sixty-seven year old uncle had said, "but sometimes you get sent on some pretty crappy missions. Sometimes covering some politicians' asses who are too stupid or pig-headed to do the right thing, and you're out there holding the line between justified civil disobedience and so called 'righteous' society—those folks who refuse to recognize that it's time for a change. I've told you before: I was there at Kent State when the Guard gunned down unarmed students who were protesting the Vietnam War. I've seen what the Guard is capable of. I lost a friend that day."

Uncle Ken's words echoed in Paul's head every time he lifted his weapon. He heard them every time he felt its cold steel. They resonated each time he slapped in an ammunition clip.

A movement below caught Paul's attention. It was Jasper, climbing the stairs toward him, his camo uniform looking more like pajamas than military attire, draped casually over his larger than average frame. The name on the uniform read Wolgamuth, but everyone referred to Brad by his nickname. Recently relocated from Wyoming, Jasper was a friendly cowboy, and Paul liked him best of all the members of his squad. He reasoned that his large, strong body might also recommend Jasper should they ever get in a tight spot.

"Break time, Swish," Jasper said, squeezing past Paul on the narrow catwalk to allow him access to the stairs. "Swish" was the nickname Paul had been given following an exercise break on a basketball court where Paul had consistently sunk basket after basket with "nothing but net." He was never sure whether it was also recognition of his sexual orientation, although he was sure he hadn't revealed that information through word or action. The name had never been used pejoratively, and that eased Paul's fears. Still, it was the kind of thing that could lead to misunderstandings and worse. But Paul's efforts to free himself from the appellation had been unsuccessful, and he had given up trying.

"Okay, Jasper. You keep a lid on things 'til I get back, ya hear?" Paul joked.

"That shouldn't be too hard," the big man answered, a large grin revealing two missing teeth, lost in a bar fight or a rodeo accident, Paul had forgotten which.

Paul descended the stairs, locked the gate behind him, and then walked the sidewalk to a small parking area near the toll plaza where the Humvee was parked. He could see Sterno asleep in the front passenger seat.

"Rise and shine, Sleeping Beauty," he said, opening the door.

Dennis Stearns was a compact man, smaller even than Paul, but with rock-solid muscles and not a pinch of paunch. A veteran of Iraq, the men of his unit looked up to him as result of his military experience. Paul would not have minded partnering with him, but Hairdo and Sterno were tight, and Paul knew his place in the pecking order. He also recognized his inferior position in the squad as the one that needed to be protected, the squad's weakest link.

Sterno released little more than a grunt and surrendered his seat in the Humvee. He spoke seldom and acted conservatively. Paul suspected it was such behavior that had insured his survival in a real military campaign.

"Be sure to relieve Hairdo at oh-eight-thirty," Stearns said as he slapped his cap on his head and slung his rifle over his shoulder. He didn't wait for a response as he turned and started walking for the bridge.

"Yes, sir," Paul said in a soft voice. Quickly realizing he was nearly inaudible, Paul repeated the reply more loudly. But Sterno was on the move, and the distance and the traffic noise combined to make him unheard again. Shrugging his shoulders, Paul climbed into the Humvee and quickly assumed the most comfortable reclining position he knew. After several weeks of rotating through this detail, he was quite familiar with what maximum comfort was available.

His three comrades and he were the standard members of this squad, and they worked well together. One extra stripe gave Sterno commanding authority, but the formality was not needed given the respect he garnered and the equanimity with which the other three spurned command responsibility. Thomas Wiggins, known as "Hairdo" either because his surname contained the word "wig" or his cleanly shaven head was a sarcastic counter-play, was the fourth member. He and Jasper had joined the Guard at about the same time, about nine months before Paul. None of the four had expected Guard duty to take up so much of their time, but two circumstances now dictated that it would. First, the declaration of martial law introduced many more responsibilities. Secondly, several of the units stationed at neighboring armories had been activated for service in Israel. Compared to an overseas deployment, these four were happy to have even this increased level of state-side duty.

Paul minded the least. Laid off two years ago from his job as a machinist in a small metal fabrication company, he was happy to get out of the house and away from the dismal economic news reported constantly each day by the cable news channels. Standing all day on guard duty wasn't much different from standing in front of a milling machine. The paychecks the Guard provided helped, too. They surpassed Justin's wages as an overnight shelf stocker at ShopRite, but the combined earnings were enough to allow Mr. Robinson and Mr. Vick to live comfortably enough. That comfort and their love for each other made for happiness.

Paul closed his eyes and recalled just a few hours earlier.

"I never could resist a man in uniform," Justin

had joked as he had pushed Paul onto the bed. Justin could be incredibly strong at times.

Paul had just lain there this time, passively and selfishly enjoying the moment. That was the most beautiful thing about their relationship. They played off each other perfectly. There never was even a hint of resentment or jealousy between them, and they were totally compatible and content with each other's love making techniques and attitudes, even as they changed over time or in different circumstances.

Paul had brought Justin home from a bar two years ago, and they had been together ever since. Besides his easygoing personality, Paul had appreciated how Justin used words to so effectively convey his emotions and feelings. Paul also quickly came to appreciate that Justin's mouth was not limited to expressing sensual sounds.

Such had been the case earlier this morning. Justin's affections had resulted in Paul attaining complete release and collapsing into perfect peace. So fully had he dissolved into that blissful state that he was hard pressed to get back into uniform and make it to the armory on time.

And with those thoughts Paul dropped off into the first of three ten-minute cat naps—the kind that provided quick bursts of refreshment without lapsing into indulgence. The kind that would not keep him from relieving Hairdo at the appointed time.

What ...
> ***[Deleted]***
>> *.... fickle*

Emily Dickinson, from No. 1195 Lines 1-4

4

Linda's breath puffed against his chest, there for a second, and gone. Michael felt it and was in awe of how slight it was, almost unnoticeable. This essential requirement for life was so dainty, so fleeting, so fragile.

She was asleep now. Her head on his shoulder had morphed into dead weight, as had her leg, draped across his. Moments before, she had been very awake, high above him, riding his phallus with a deliberate cadence and consuming passion that led to an inevitable conclusion. Hints of approaching morning daylight slipped through gaps in the curtains and highlighted her long brown hair that cascaded over her shoulders and down her back. He smiled as he remembered their first time when they had done it literally over the head and figuratively under the nose of his uncle, upstairs in his cabin on Lake Wallenpaupack. She had been more energetic then—and more vocal, as he recalled his difficulty in silencing her in that loft. Though their lovemaking may have become more sedate in its mechanics over the years, it seemed more satisfying, more fulfilling. He knew he loved her more today than ever before. No other woman tempted him, for he had seen none more beautiful than his wife.

When he thought about how he had nearly lost her, he trembled. Five years had passed, but he remembered the time as though it were last week. He had apologized honestly and completely, but her reaction had been understandable.

"What do you mean, you don't know what you were thinking?' she had demanded. "You must have been thinking something!"

"No sooner had I left the apartment than I felt miserable, ashamed," was his weak response.

"You should have been ashamed! You destroyed the place!"

"The rage—for the life of me I don't know what set me off—but once it started, I couldn't stop. And right after, I'm thinking: I'm not mad at her, I'm mad at what she did. And then I couldn't remember *that*! Oh, certain little things, like a look you'd give a guy that would make me insane with jealousy. But nothing that would justify me getting so angry, that it would cause me to risk losing you."

"It hurt, Mike. It really did. What you did to things—*our* things—it felt like you were attacking me. I wondered what would have happened to me if I had been there."

"No, Lin, I could never hurt you. Never physically, never intentionally."

"I want to believe you, Mike. I really do. But I'm scared."

"Take me back. Please. I'll make it up to you, I promise. I love you."

She had taken him back. And she never mentioned the incident again—while Michael remembered it daily.

"Whatcha thinkin'?" she asked, looking up at him without lifting her head, her fingertips caressing his chest.

He looked down into her brown eyes, now large and alert. "Thinking how much I love you," he said.

"Mmmm."

"Do you still love me, Linda?"

"Nah, you're just my first trick of the day. You gotta clear out before my eight o'clock gets here." She bit her lower lip as she smiled at her own joke. When he accepted the challenge in her eyes, she struggled to pin him, their interlaced fingers flailing about in an effort to gain or thwart an advantage. In time, he overpowered her, flipping her on her back and bringing his forehead down to touch hers as she breathed heavily from the exertion. Then he closed the distance until his mouth found hers, and his question was satisfactorily answered.

I ...
   [Deleted]
         ... see –

Emily Dickinson, from No. 563 Lines 9-12

5

"Aren't you going to eat anything?" Michael asked, as Linda marshaled her satchel, laptop, and assorted bags in preparation for departure.

"No. I'll grab a donut and a coffee on the way," she replied.

"Yeah, that sounds healthy."

"Cut me some slack. It's not like I do it all the time."

"All five days this week. Sounds like a pattern to me."

"Yeah, well I just don't have the time. This semester is off to a crazy start already. And it didn't help that you kept me in bed this morning." Linda directed her voice into the hallway and shouted, "Lizzy!! Are you up?"

"Well, I can't help it if you're so sexy," Michael said, pouring some milk onto his breakfast cereal.

"That's gross!" exclaimed Liz, entering the kitchen before her mother's call finished echoing up the central staircase.

"Your mother is not gross, Liz," Michael countered.

"I can't believe you guys are still doing it," said Liz, peeling a banana as she moved through the kitchen. Repeatedly she was in the way of her mother who was becoming more frantic in collecting some textbooks left on the counter.

"And why not?" Michael asked. "The act doesn't seem to keep you from wanting to see those R-rated movies. What makes those actors different?"

"Well, for one thing, they're not fossilized," Liz said. "Dad, can I have twenty bucks?"

"Twenty dollars—again? Didn't I just give you money earlier this week?"

"That's gone. Prices are going up everywhere: pizza, the movies. The bus fare went up fifty cents again."

"No kidding. Which is why your mother and I just can't keep pouring cash into your pocket every time we see you. And we are not fossilized, I'll have you know."

"I'm off. I'll see you later," Linda interjected. "What time are you done tonight, Liz?"

"I'm on 'til nine. I should be home by ten if the bus is on time. Can't wait until I get my own car."

"Like you'll be able to afford to put gas in it" Michael said, digging into his pants pocket for his wallet. "Have a good one, Linda."

"Bye, Mom."

"Bye, guys," Linda said as she stepped out the door.

"Bye, Dad," Liz said, taking the offered twenty dollar bill and moving towards the same door where her mother just left.

"That's it? Just a banana for breakfast?"

"I'm late. And I've got a test first period. No time. Thanks. Bye!"

With that, she was gone, leaving Michael alone in the quiet house. Alone with his thoughts. Alone with his fears. Michael had his share. When his specialty butcher shop and delicatessen had gone bankrupt, Michael had already sunk a sizable amount of his personal cash to keep the operation afloat. Satisfying the creditors had left nothing over to repay his interest, and his family had suffered. Only Linda's job at the high school had kept them solvent, allowed them to pay the mortgage and to keep the house.

Now, in his latest venture, another meat business, he was beginning to show profits, having reached the break-even point sooner than he had expected. But this success came at a price.

Michael went behind the garage and yanked the tarpaulin off the truck parked there, and disconnected the electric cord that powered the refrigeration unit. He was probably being too cautious to cover the truck with the tarp each night, but then he wondered if he could be too cautious. Too bad the truck wouldn't fit into the garage. That would make it much easier. He climbed into the cab and started the truck, then quickly pulled around the garage and into the street. Two more turns and he was immersed in the morning rush-hour traffic.

He drove east on Route 46 from Garfield to Palisades Park, where he went north on Grand Avenue to his first stop, a trendy restaurant in Tenafly. Pulling around back, he gave the bell by the door two short rings. Not much later, Sal came out, and Michael shoved up the rear door.

"How's it going?" Michael asked, still not comfortable with attempting familiarity.

"It goes. Whadaya got for me today?" Sal responded, not making Michael feel any easier.

"Prime ribs, sirloin, some ground round. Some real nice veal, some legs of lamb. No pork, today—a problem up the supply chain."

"Yeah, and what's this gonna run me?"

"A pound and a half."

"You shittin' me?"

"Sorry, man. That's the deal. You're my first stop. If you're not interested, I'll head up the road. I *will* return home empty." Michael reached up for the strap to pull the door closed.

"Hold on. Not so fast, Mike. We'll do

business. I just didn't expect another price hike."

"Outta my control, man."

"Yeah, yeah, I know. This stuff is USDA approved, right?"

"It's all stamped."

"That's not what I asked."

"It's all stamped," Mike repeated.

"A little bird told me this stuff comes outa Canada."

"I don't ask many questions," Mike said. "You should do the same. We gonna do this?"

Sal reached into his pocket and pulled out a wad of bills, then peeled off the requisite number and handed them to Michael.

"Okay," Michael said, and began shoving Sal's order onto the lift gate.

It dropped so low – in my Regard –
I heard it hit the Ground

Emily Dickinson, from No. 747

6

Rufus let out a bark and ran towards the front door. Russell looked at the clock and sighed. Nine-thirty. His time in the morning at home was about finished. Time to get moving. He shut off Fox News and compacted the recliner as the doorbell rang. Rufus let out two more barks.

It was FedEx. The girl's face was cute, her short blond hair framing it nicely. But something—the jaunty angle at which she wore her ball cap, the bright green gum she snapped in her teeth, or maybe her legs which her purple uniform shorts revealed to be very muscular—one of those things ruined the image. Russell wasn't looking for anything for himself, but quietly longed to see some femininity in her.

Russell signed for the package, standing in the doorway to keep Rufus at bay. He turned back into the house and ripped the box open. He emptied the contents onto the stairs: three holsters for his Glock.

Returning to the family room, Russell retrieved the weapon from his briefcase and tried it in each of the three holsters. It fit well into each of them. Firm. Secure. He stepped into the powder room and flipped on the light, Rufus following close behind. In front of the mirror Russell tried on the shoulder holster. The elastic grabbed at his armpits. He adjusted it. It still grabbed. He would have to get used to that. Checking the mirror, he noted that this choice would keep the weapon high and concealed—

provided he wore a sport coat. But he couldn't take the coat off. That might be a problem.

Next, he strapped the ankle holster to his lower right calf. It felt awkward, strange. He raised his pant leg and holstered the Glock. The weight made him feel unbalanced. He pulled up his pant leg and drew the gun. Clumsy. Still, he wasn't expecting a quick-draw situation. This choice seemed to offer quite a bit of concealment, though he'd have to be careful about casually sitting with his ankle on his knee.

Finally, he placed the gun in the inside-the-pants holster, and slipped them together inside his waist band on his left hip. He slipped the holster's clip over his belt, a heavy belt he had recently purchased, anticipating this need. His recent weight loss provided plenty of space, and feeling the gun's barrel against his upper thigh was strangely reassuring. Then he wondered how much it would truly hurt if he shot his ass off.

He had read in a gun magazine about the loss of time when cross drawing a weapon across your body. So he shifted the gun to his right hip. But Russell didn't like the way the grip protruded to the rear. He returned it to its original position, where the stock was cradled by the softness of his abdomen. Then he puffed his shirt out of his pants to cover the grip, tucking a bit of shirt tail under the holster clip. He turned several times in front of the mirror, satisfied with the gun's concealment. Russell removed the two empty holsters. He was ready to go.

The ride to the college was uneventful. The traffic on Interstate 80 was always heavy eastbound—the shoppers, the delivery trucks, commuters to late starting jobs. Russell could never predict how the drive from Parsippany would go. Sometimes it was easy sailing. Often times he encountered accidents or traffic backed up for no apparent reason. He always allowed himself more than enough time, and if he was late, his first commitment was office hours, so tardiness would not impact too many.

His mind was lost in the muddle he experienced when driving in heavy traffic. Mid-terms were next week, but that did not concern him. He assigned enough essays to meet any grading needs. His essay critiques would be more important to his students than an "A" or a "B" on a multiple choice test. Lenny had asked him something yesterday. What was it? Whatever it was, he'd ask again. Then Russell's ears perked up when he heard the radio news story.

"Yet another student was assaulted on the campus of Schuyler University last night. Authorities said the nineteen-year-old woman was unharmed after being accosted by two males in a robbery attempt. They were reportedly armed with knives. This is the fourth such incident at the college during the first six weeks of classes."

He reached down and clenched the grip of the handgun. He felt relieved, a comfort in knowing he carried protection.

Russell found his usual parking space in the far corner of the faculty lot. Getting out of the car, he felt the weight of the gun exerting downward pressure on his pants. He pulled them up and wished he could cinch his belt tighter, but he was out of holes. He walked to the Mansion, keenly aware of his secret in his waistband.

* * * *

Russell was reading his email messages when he heard a soft knock on his office door.

"Professor Grayson?" It was Leonard Rudolph, Dean of the College of Liberal Arts. Tall and thin, with pure white hair combed straight back over his head, Lenny was as comfortable in his role at Schuyler as he would be uncomfortable doing anything else. Beside him stood a short, balding man, whose small eyes set deep in their sockets were encircled by the large lenses of his eyeglasses. Russell recognized him from photographs as the man who had been hired to take his wife's position at the university.

"Come in, Lenny."

"Russell, I'd like you to meet Martin Fitzsimmons, our new professor of economics."

"How do you do, Martin," Russell said, extending his hand.

"Marty, please," corrected the newcomer. His handshake was firm, and his left hand soon joined his right to surround Russell's. "May I extend my sincere condolences? Please understand how difficult I find this meeting under these circumstances."

"Thank you," Russell responded.

Lenny quickly interjected, Russell guessed to lighten the tone, for Lenny was the consummate conciliator. "Marty brings a great deal of experience to Schuyler. He served as an economic advisor to President Obama; he's written two books. His latest, on price controls, was on the *Times*' best seller list for over a month."

"I've read your treatise on Milton Friedman," Russell volunteered.

"Really? I'm impressed," Marty said, smiling. "Not too many English professors delve into 'the dismal science'."

"Being married to an economist for twenty-five years can do that to a fellow."

"And what did you think of it?" Marty asked, his smile lingering, his head assuming a slight tilt.

"I found it a bit harsh, frankly. I met the man a few years before he died. A very decent human being. Some of your assumptions regarding his motivations just don't hold up, I'm afraid."

"Well, that's the good thing about academia," Lenny cut in again, "we have the ability to disagree peacefully in pursuit of the truth."

"You were aware that Meredith subscribed to the Chicago School?" Russell asked Marty.

"Yes, yes I was. But I never let our political differences prevent me from appreciating her intellect or some of the profound things she wrote."

"Even though she was working to undo everything that Obama created and that Benson is perpetuating?"

"Even so," Marty answered, his tiny eyes, magnified by his glasses, focused on Russell's face.

Russell stared back, looking for a sign of sincerity. He wasn't sure he saw one. "Well, welcome to Schuyler. If I can assist you in any way, please let me know."

"Thank you, Russell," Marty said.

"Well, then," said Lenny, "we have a few more introductions to make. If you'll excuse us, Russell?"

* * * *

It was no secret that Russell ate lunch at this small coffee shop, just off campus, nearly every day. That Lenny should show up here could not be accidental.

"May I join you?" Lenny asked, motioning to a seat across from where Russell was sitting.

"Of course." Russell sat at his usual corner table, close to the window so he had light to read. With Lenny's approach, though, he had closed his book and moved his lunch to decrease his claim to the table's surface.

"I must say, you didn't make that encounter any easier," Lenny said, unwrapping his sandwich.

"The man asked my opinion. I was honest."

"That you were. And you wasted no time in highlighting your political differences."

"He knew them coming in. As did I. We just

marked our territory."

"Like two dogs pissing on tree stumps."

"Now why do you want to insult dogs?"

"But really, Russell, couldn't it have waited? The very first day?"

"It could have been completely avoided. I told you right away I was disappointed the committee was considering Fitzsimmons. I felt—still feel—it's a slap at Meredith to hire a socialist to replace her. After all she did! She put Schuyler on the map, for crying out loud. No one had ever heard of Schuyler until Landers started quoting her. Now the admissions office is overwhelmed with applications."

"He is not a 'socialist.'"

"Oh, please, don't label him as a 'Keynesian'. J.M.K. would roll over in his grave if he knew how his name had been hijacked by so many statists."

"Maybe you should consider changing your field to economics."

Russell chose not to respond to that comment, taking a bite of his sandwich instead. After he swallowed, he assumed a more conciliatory tone.

"Hey, I'm still pretty new to this stuff. But when your stock portfolio goes south in less than a week, the value of your home plummets, and you don't see a raise in your paycheck for several years—yeah, I take an interest in economics. I was fortunate to be sleeping with a damned good economist."

"It's just an economic cycle. We'll pull out of it eventually."

"That's bull, Lenny. Look at the shortages in the stores. Look at the crime rate. Hell, we had another assault on campus last night! And the kids. I keep looking at these fresh faces and try to offer them hope for the future. Meanwhile I've got graduates from six years ago who come back to visit—bright kids—working dead-end jobs. Something has to change, and soon. And this martial law crap—that's the only way Benson can hold on to power. The voters would throw him out on his ear in a heartbeat."

"I'm older than you, Russell. I tend to look at things with a more historic perspective. During the Great Depression, people thought it was pretty bleak. But we came out of it, and experienced one of the greatest economic booms ever."

"With the help of a World War," Russell countered. "Which, by the way, is what we nearly have in the Middle East, where Karen probably is, thank you, very much."

"Karen's deployed there?"

"I don't know for sure. The Air Force is extremely secretive these days, and she won't say anything, but it makes sense. F-15's are leading the attack, and that's what she flies."

"Russ, I'm sorry. My prayers are with her."

"Thanks, Lenny."

"Just try to be a little nicer to Marty, okay?" Lenny was standing, rolling up his sandwich wrapper and sticking it in his soft drink cup. "He's not with the Administration any longer."

"No," smiled Russell, "the rats always know when to get off the ship."

*I ... **[Deleted]***
　　... smile –
　　　　　　Emily Dickinson, from No. 223 Lines 1-2

7

Liz stood under the bus stop shelter, her school books weighing down the day pack slung over her shoulder. She hated this trip. The three block walk from school to the bus stop, the waiting, hoping for a seat once the bus arrived—all combined for a dismal experience. The Hispanic woman seated behind her stared forward blankly; she had hardly acknowledged Liz's smile and greeting. *Certainly it hadn't been that hard to translate,* Liz thought. Outside the clear plastic booth, a blond-haired man just a few years older than her paced impatiently back and forth, stepping into the street occasionally to take a better look for the bus. He carried a thin portfolio under his arm, and that, and his tapered blue suit, gave him an air of importance.

At last the bus arrived, squeaking and hissing to a stop, the doors swinging violently open. The blond-haired man was standing directly in front of the steps when the bus stopped, and sprang aboard when he was allowed entry, only to retreat back to the sidewalk to enable a disembarking woman to exit. He jumped on again, and as Liz prepared to follow, the silent woman on the bench stepped in front of her and climbed the steps. Dipping her ten-trip ticket into the reader, Liz scanned the bus for seats. There were two. One was an aisle seat into which the Hispanic woman plopped. The other was the seat directly behind the driver, where a disheveled man half sat, half lay, sound asleep, his mouth agape displaying some discolored teeth. Reluctantly, she perched on the corner of the seat the man's outstretched body left unoccupied.

Liz placed her book bag between her feet, being careful not to extend into the aisle. She removed her biology book and turned to the marked page listing the animal classes, and resumed the memorization process: *Cnidaria - sea anemones, corals, and jellyfish; Annelida - segmented worms; Mollusca - clams, snails, and squids;...* Her seat companion snorted, jerked abruptly, and let out a long sigh during which he wiped his mouth with the sleeve of his shirt. Through all of these sounds and actions he did not awake. Liz regarded him, pondering where he might come to rest in her listing of phyla.

A bank of clouds moving in from the west masked the sun as Liz got off the bus at the strip mall where she worked. It was a short walk across the parking lot to the store, which sold women's clothing. Although they pretended to be a trendy store, the Williamson's chain was much more main-stream than some of the boutiques in the area. But some of the styles matched Liz's tastes, and she exercised her employee discount frequently to supplement her own wardrobe.

"Hi Liz," Marci said, looking up from the paperwork she was completing next to the cash register.

"Hey."

"There's a shipment in the back we got in today. Haven't had a chance to touch it."

"Okay, I'll get on it. Is Gail coming in?"

"No. She called out. It's just you and me."

Liz stashed her pack in the store's back room and checked the schedule. She groaned softly and returned to the sales floor.

"What happened to my hours next week?" she asked Marci.

"Everyone's being cut back. A home office

decision. They should come back in a few weeks. You know, Black Friday, the holidays."

"I was really counting on those hours. I need to make some money before Christmas."

"Sorry. It's not my idea."

Liz sighed and returned to the back room to grab the clothes that had just arrived. She rolled the cart loaded with cardboard cartons to the sportswear section, and began hanging shirts on the racks. She knew Marci had little control over her hours. As a manager, she just placed names in the blocks the corporate office sent her. She didn't play favorites, but just about everything was controlled by people outside the store, with a weekly visit by the Regional Manger to make sure that directions were being followed.

Still, Liz knew how lucky she was to even have a job, and this one was better than many others. Most of her friends at school couldn't find jobs. Some had lost the jobs they had when large chain stores had laid off thousands of part-time workers following the recent hike in the Minimum Wage. Not that Liz made minimum wage—Williamson's, she had been told, was exempt due to a provision of the Wage and Price Control Act.

* * * *

The afternoon dripped into evening, one minute at a time. Liz worked like a programmed robot. She'd break into a box—being careful with her fingernails—and hang or stack the garments for display. She had mastered the skill of folding a top or a pair of jeans with the least number of movements in the shortest amount of time. Her motions were automatic, freeing her mind for other things. *What did Chris really think of her? Did he love her? Did she love him? She sure thought she did. But how could she be sure? She had never felt this way before, but was it for real? What was college going to be like? What was college going to be like without Chris? What was she going to buy him for Christmas? And with the hours being cut, would she be able to buy him much of anything?*

"Do you have this in a size seven?" The customer held up a long sleeve sweater for Liz to see.

"Let me look," Liz said, switching on her "customer service" smile.

"You don't seem to have the selection you used to have," the woman continued.

"We just got some things in; I'm putting them out now." Liz knew the woman was right, though. Several racks had been taken off the floor "to give the store a more spacious look". However, it was clear the amount of inventory was down—and the number of frustrated customers was up. "I'm sorry, it looks like we're out of that size. I can order it for you, though."

"Don't bother," the woman said, her frustration not hidden at all.

* * * *

"I need you to have that cart empty by close," Marci said. She had left Liz alone for most of the evening. Now, with closing time less than two hours away, she was focusing on achieving goals. Whenever she tried to play her manager role it was a complete change from her usual co-worker attitude.

"I'll get it done," said Liz. Unlike some of the others, Liz never mocked Marci. She appreciated her friendship too much.

"You sure? You seem a little slow, today. Like you're distracted."

Liz had been trying to stay focused, but clearly she hadn't been very successful. After three hours, the boxes on the cart still far outnumbered those set aside to be recycled. She had skipped her break in an effort to compensate. "I'm okay," she countered.

"Really?"

There was little chance of fooling Marci. "Oh, I've got some stuff on my mind. A guy, mostly."

"At your age, it usually is."

At just a few years older, Marci was always portraying herself as older and more experienced. For her willingness to listen, Liz always honored her illusion. "It's Chris," Liz said, "sometimes he seems so into me, and then sometimes he won't call me for a week."

"That's the way guys are: flakey, easily distracted. Then, when you bring it to their attention, it's 'Aw, you're making it too much of a big deal.'"

"Exactly! But if you even *talk* to another guy, he gets all upset, like 'What are you talking to him for? I thought you and me had something special.' All defensive-like. Really jealous."

"Yeah, your Chris sounds about normal."

"Then there are the times we're alone together: it's so perfect. He cares so much, and shows it. It's like I can't imagine anybody else in his place."

"Known that feeling…several times."

"But if one of his friends shows up, he's gotta be cool. He has to impress his pal by showing that I'm not all that important, even making fun of me if that makes it more convincing."

"That's the way they roll, honey. You can play along, or you can play alone."

"It just pisses me off, sometimes."

"Yeah, well eventually they come to their senses. They settle down a little bit. Just remember, they will *always* be boys."

A **[Deleted]**
... understood –

Emily Dickinson, from No. 719 Lines 5-6

8

Linda looked into the paper bag at the half-eaten blueberry donut. It was not appealing in the least. When she brought the Styrofoam cup to her lips, the coffee was stone cold. She sighed. She could use an energy boost now, but she wasn't that desperate. She would have to wait until lunch, three periods away.

"Hi, Linda," Matt Ferguson greeted her as he entered the teacher's lounge. Being a fastidious dresser, his trim frame produced a neat, organized appearance. When most of the faculty wore jeans, he still wore sport jackets and tailored pants. As he usually did, he placed his satchel on a table and stepped to the copy machine to prepare handouts for his Algebra classes.

"Hey, Matt. How's it going?"

"Same old," he replied. "How about you?"

"Hectic. I just can't seem to get on top of things this year. The faster I go, the more I get behind."

"Teacher's convention in a couple of weeks. Maybe you can catch your breath then."

"Yeah, but I've got a workshop the following week. And you know how that is, you're out of the building for a day and it takes three to catch up."

"Mmm. Where's the workshop?" he asked.

"It's at Drew. A symposium on teaching literature."

"I can imagine that could go either way—interesting insights or booorrring."

"Yeah, you're right. Too often, it's the latter. But Susan signed me up. Said I needed to get out and pick up some C.E.U.'s. Haven't been doing much of that the last few years. And you know me; I don't want to be the one to drag down the professionalism of the Wallington High School staff!"

Matt chuckled. "You're way down on that list, Linda."

Linda smiled a thank you. She and Matt were mutual admirers, seasoned teachers who commiserated with each other regarding the natural frustrations and bureaucratic offences inherent in the profession.

"Did you see yesterday's memo from Napoleon?" Matt asked.

Linda tried to hide her amusement at Matt's nickname for their tall, lanky, red-headed principal, fiendishly nicknamed, Napoleon Dynamite. "The one on the teacher evaluations?" she asked.

"Uh-huh."

"Yeah, I saw it. So we're going to be judged by two rounds of tests?"

"That's right. The fall test will be the set up for the spring 'final exam'. Sort of an early warning system so the administration can start early on the replacement hiring process."

"It's ridiculous that so much weight can be put on a standardized test," Linda offered. "And direct observation of what's going in the classroom—that's a thing of the past."

"We're just interchangeable cogs on the gears, Linda," Matt said. "If the test says you're not efficient, off you go, replaced by another cog just like you—at least on paper. The thing is, there are thousands of influences on student performance. But they're all ignored. If a group of students does poorly, it *has* to be the teacher's fault, and his alone."

"This administration was supposed to be pro-teacher," Linda added. "But our jobs get more difficult and less appreciated. Now it's getting harder to hold on to them, too."

"And what happened to our pensions? That was criminal."

"Doesn't stop the NJEA from endorsing them for re-election. You notice that?"

"Year after year," Matt said with resignation.

* * * *

"Brad," said Linda, calling on the tall boy in the rear of the classroom, "why is Brutus reluctant to join Cassius and the others?"

"I dunno," replied the boy, slouching in his chair to diminish his size. His scarlet varsity jacket would make him stand out in any room, regardless of his physique.

"Did you read Act I?" she asked.

"I tried, Ms Norton, but it didn't make much sense."

"But I'm sure you understood something in your reading. Build on what you know."

"I can't," Brad said, his head turned down towards his desk.

"Tell me, Brad, have you ever been involved in a busted play during a football game?"

"Sure."

"When that happens, do you and your teammates just stop dead still and stand there?"

"No way! We'd get killed!"

"Exactly. So what does the team do?"

"We run the play the best we can. Whoever has the ball tries to run toward the goal."

"Good. Now *you've* got the ball. I'm not suggesting any fatal consequences in this classroom, but I would like to see you 'run toward the goal.'"

Brad grunted his understanding.

"So, what do you know about Brutus. Who does he like? Who does he love?"

"He says he loves Caesar: 'I would not, Cassius; yet I love him well.'"

"Good start! Who else?"

"Cassius. I saw it here somewhere…"

"'But let not therefore my good friends be grieved

Among which number, Cassius, be you one'"

"Yeah, that's it."

"But what are Cassius's feelings towards Caesar?" Linda asked.

"He wants to kill him."

"Right! And what does that create for Brutus?"

"A conflict?"

"You think? Rachel, how does Brutus feel about Rome?"

Unproved   ***[Deleted]***
           ... fear –

Emily Dickinson, from No. 1202 Lines 21-22

9

Russell entered his office to see the phone message stuck on his computer screen. The name Anna Marston was vaguely familiar, and then he remembered, with an accompanying sinking feeling in his gut, that last spring she had recruited him for a literature symposium the following year. He uncovered his diary from under a pile of papers on his desk and flipped it open to November. There it was, circled twice, the date just a few weeks away, and for which he had prepared absolutely nothing. He moaned aloud.

As he now recalled, it was to be a roundtable discussion with two or three other college professors and about three times as many high school teachers. That suggested the possibility for a great deal of *ad lib* pontificating. *That shouldn't require a great deal of preparation,* he thought. *Still, he had made a commitment, and he should honor it by doing some preparation work. Right, so he'd call her back tomorrow when he could honestly say that he had been working on it, since to be honest today, he would have to admit that the conference had been totally forgotten.*

He returned the sticky note to a prominent place on his computer screen, and sat down to review the few pieces of mail he had found in his faculty mail box. He swiveled in his chair to make access to the waste basket more convenient, when the phone rang.

"Good afternoon, this is Professor Grayson," he said.

"Professor Grayson, I have some information on your wife's murder." The male voice was deep in tone and slightly muffled. "If you'd rather not hear it, I would understand, and will not bother you again. If you want to hear it, well, I'm willing to provide it."

"Who is this?" Russell asked. This had all the earmarks of a prank call from someone with a really sick mind, but something about it had a ring of sincerity. He was tempted to hang up even as his curiosity was aroused.

"I'm afraid I can't reveal that. That will be a condition of our conversations—I must have total anonymity. You can't ask for further details. If I learn that you've tried to find out who I am—and I have ways to find out—I will take extreme steps to protect myself and discredit you. Is that clear?"

"Why such secrecy?" Russell asked.

"I'm taking extraordinary risks contacting you," the voice said. "The repercussions for me could be devastating—possibly fatal. Again, I won't take any more risks than I already have."

"You have to see this sounds awfully strange to me," Russell said

"I appreciate that. I am prepared to offer you proof of my authenticity, but I need to know you understand the ground rules, first."

"Then why are you doing this?"

"Let's just say I took an oath once, and that oath was important to me."

"An oath to whom?"

"Again, I can't say." Russell detected a note of annoyance in the voice. He was, however, hooked by the mysterious caller's pitch.

"Okay. I think I understand your rules, though I'm not sure of your motivation."

"All right, then. Your wife, John Landers,

John Grissom, Brenda Harris, Stephen Zuckerman—all were murdered in a well-planned attack by a team of five men."

Russell digested this information, while the voice paused. The names were public information; the number of attackers was news to Russell. "The video tapes only show three men," Russell asserted.

"There were two others that never entered the gymnasium. Among other things, they drove the getaway vehicles." The voice possessed an air of authority that only worked to draw Russell in deeper.

"Have you informed the Secret Service of this?" Russell asked.

"Who? Burns? He's busy protecting the Service whose job it was to protect Landers. The Secret Service and the F.B.I. have these leads and more, but are choosing not to pursue them."

Russell had met Burns, who had reached out to him soon after the attack. The caller did appear to be close to the investigation if he knew Burns. "Why would they do that?" Russell questioned.

"Why does anyone do anything? Motivations. I'm not sure what they are, but my gut feeling is that they're sinister. I don't want to believe that, but I'm finding few viable alternatives. That's why I'm calling you. I need your help."

"My help?"

"Yes. I need you to put some pressure on the investigators. As a relative of one of the victims, they'll listen to you. At least to a point. But again, you cannot tell *anyone* that you spoke to me."

"Yeah, I got that. You said they were ignoring other leads?"

"That's right. Investigators reviewed passenger lists for airline flights around the time of the attack. Five two-bit hoodlums from Paterson flew into Terre Haute, Indianapolis, and Dayton, three days before the murders. They flew back to Newark, again from various airports, two to four days after the attack. Rather coincidental, don't you think?"

"Yeah, I suppose so."

"Right. But there were no follow-up interviews of any of them. The request of the Newark office to do so was quashed by someone high in the Bureau. 'An unnecessary waste of resources' it was said. In an assassination investigation? Do you believe that?"

"But why?"

"That's the million dollar question. Procedure would dictate questioning them. Eliminate them if they have alibis; focus on them if they don't."

"And what do you think I can do?"

"I'm not really sure. I've been kicking this around for some time. Anyway, the guys working on the case pressed for the follow-up. A day or so later, they received a brief report from Newark clearing these slime balls. But get this, one of them makes a follow-up phone call to the agent who signed the report, and he denies conducting the interview! Knows nothing about it! So the Indiana guy alerts his boss, who says he'll look into it. A few hours later, the agent in Jersey calls back, 'Oh yeah,' he says, 'my mistake. I did that interview. He's clean.' 'Really?' says Indiana, 'you *forgot* about an interview involving the biggest crime of the year?!?' To which Jersey hems and haws and cuts the call short because 'he's real busy.'

"This stinks to high heaven," the voice continued. "For the Jersey agent to play along suggests a *lot* of pressure was applied. So Indiana goes back to his boss, who's ticked that he didn't let him handle it, and piles on assignments of following-up bullshit leads to nowhere. Whoever thought this up didn't expect the agents to talk to each other, and when they did the whole thing fell apart. Now they're scrambling to cover it all up. Another independent inquiry might really throw them off balance."

"But how am I supposed to know about this, if

I haven't talked to you?" Russell was sure now that the caller was some kind of an investigator of the murders.

"Yeah, I know, I haven't got an answer for that yet. It's pretty clear that any more follow-up by the Indiana agent is going to have serious repercussions for him. That's why I thought it would be better coming from outside the Bureau. But let me warn you, what's going down is high-stakes stuff. I'm willing to bet whoever is behind this will take extreme measures to cover their asses. Your involvement could mean a great deal of risk. You hearing me?"

"Loud and clear."

"Okay, I'll give you some time to think about it. I'll call you again."

And with that, the phone went dead.

Low ... ***[Deleted]***
... comes –
Emily Dickinson, from No. 69 Lines 1-2

10

Michael snaked his way through the streets of Paterson, past the lines of dirty row houses, past the idle young men hacking around on the street corners. He squeezed the truck through streets constricted by double parked cars and stopped to wait patiently as a woman, pushing a baby stroller and leading a youngster by the hand, stepped in front of him without so much as a glance in his direction. The little girl in tow, wearing a stained red coat, looked up at him with a blank expression that belied the wonder of childhood.

He swung the truck beneath the archway that led into the industrial center. Once a large chemical manufacturing complex, the old brick buildings with their tall arched windows had been subdivided years before. Today, the complex offered tenancies to numerous warehousing and small-scale manufacturing concerns. He picked his way through the maze, around buildings, through cavernous alleys, splashing through huge puddles of rainwater, pausing at last to back up to a loading dock. Except for the cryptic identifier "L-7" affixed at a high corner, the building lacked any clue as to the name or activity of any operations inside.

Michael alighted from the cab and climbed a short steel stairway where he pounded on a windowless steel door. A stocky man opened it. He sported carrot-colored hair beneath a white paper cap. His ruddy complexion was matched by blood stains on the long white apron he wore over a white tee shirt. Without a word, the man stepped aside to allow Michael to enter.

"Hey, Rudy. How's it going?" was Michael's greeting.

The man in white did little more than grunt before closing the door. He led Michael into the room, his motion appearing to be more left-to-right oscillation than forward progress.

The walls were mint green in color, and the air was cool. Even beneath his wool-lined flight jacket, Michael felt his shoulders hunch in response both to the temperature and the sight of Rudy's uncovered pink arms. Long fluorescent light fixtures hung from the ceiling, illuminating the white tables below. A half dozen men, dressed like Rudy, deployed cleavers, saws, and knives on the raw meat, whole carcasses being converted to packaged single portions.

Rudy led Michael to a partitioned office in a corner. There he looked over the order Michael handed him, nodded silently, and then sat down at the desk to price it using a calculator. When finished, he showed Michael the final number on the tape, still without uttering a word. From a roll of bills in his pocket, Michael withdrew the necessary amount. With the money in his hands, Rudy motioned to two men nearby to begin loading the truck.

Working efficiently, the men soon had the truck loaded. "Thanks, Rudy!" Michael shouted from the door. Rudy returned a brief wave with his left hand without looking up, even as his right hand brought a cleaver downward with a forceful chop.

Back in the cab, Michael started to drive towards the gate. He was a few hundred feet from the packing plant when a large black sedan backed into his path. Michael came to a stop, expecting the car to shift into gear and proceed out of his way. He was a little surprised when the car's back-up lights lit for an instant and both front doors opened and two men stepped out.

The driver was tall and gaunt, wearing a black overcoat. He was hatless, displaying brown hair cut short except for a defiant clump standing erect above his brow. The passenger was stockier and wore an overcoat that could have been ordered from the same catalog as his partner's. He wore a brimmed hat which cast a shadow over his already dark complexioned face. The two men approached Michael's door with the tall man standing directly opposite while his partner lingered just beyond the truck's front fender. Nervously, Michael rolled down his window.

"Good afternoon, Mr. Norton," the tall one said.

"Have we met?" Michael asked. That his name was known to these men was a troubling development. Suddenly, he was keenly aware that the stocky one had not removed his hand from his coat pocket. Michael glanced into his rearview mirror, evaluating an escape to the rear. The route was twisted and constricted, not his choice for evasive maneuvers in a delivery truck in reverse gear.

"You are known to us," said the tall man. "Our employer would like you to join his company."

"Thanks, but I work alone."

"Joining our firm offers many benefits. Perhaps you should consider them."

So that was it, he thought, *a shakedown, more accurately, an unwanted silent partnership with the mob. Michael had heard other drivers tell of being approached in such a manner. Most of them had reluctantly acquiesced. The syndicates had many methods to encourage joining, ranging from blackmail through violence.*

"Who would be interested in this crummy little route?" Michael asked.

"We hear you do okay," the man responded.

"We'd like to help you do better."

"And you are...?"

"You can call me 'Marv.' Can I call you 'Michael?'"

"'Mr. Norton' works fine, thanks. So what's the name of your company?"

"All in due time, Michael." The man approached the truck, extending his arm to offer Michael a piece of paper. Michael hesitated a second before taking it. "Come to that address tomorrow night at eight," Marv said. "Everything will be explained to you there."

The man started to walk back towards his car, then stopped to speak over his shoulder. "Don't be late."

> And... **[Deleted]**
> ... Brain –
> Emily Dickinson, from No. 419 Lines 9-10

11

"Ugh, the time!" Russell groaned, glancing at his watch. Rufus would be ready to knock him over, for sure, the dog having been confined to the house a few hours longer than normal. The faculty meeting had dragged on, as usual, and then Russell had decided to prepare some notes for the upcoming symposium at Drew. Before he knew it, seven o'clock had come and gone.

He walked briskly out to his car. He observed the spirit, if not the letter, of the fifteen mile per hour speed limit posted on the campus drives, but accelerated with fervor as he left the college. Just a few hundred yards before the ramp to I-80, a line of traffic stood unmoving before him, all stopped before the two police cars, their overhead emergency LED units flashing in blinding pulses of red and blue.

Russell instantly thought of the Glock, and reached to his waistline to ensure by feel that the gun was hidden by his shirt. Despite confirming that this was the case, he nevertheless felt a tightening in his throat as he recognized the risk, should his secret be revealed.

"Good evening, sir. May I see your license and registration?" The officer looked young, not much older than Russell's students. Russell's eyes wandered to the automatic holstered on the cop's hip, which suddenly seemed so much larger than his own.

Russell established eye contact as he proffered

the documents, which he had fished out of wallet and glove box as the line of traffic had slowly advanced. "Certainly. Is there some sort of trouble?"

"No, sir. Just a routine credentials check, authorized by the Decree of Martial Law." The officer perused the documents before asking, "And what is your business out on the street this evening, Mr. Grayson?"

"I'm returning home from Schuyler College. I am a professor there."

"You have any college I.D.?"

"Of course." Russell removed the clip from his shirt pocket, as he had not removed the badge in his haste to leave the campus. He glanced at the photo on the identification badge. He never liked that picture; he thought his grin made him look goofy. "Here you are."

Russell was aware of the policeman's eyes darting between Russell's badge and face. He offered a sheepish grin to ease the identification process.

"Very well, Professor Grayson. Have a safe trip home."

Once on his way, Russell exhaled a long breath of relief. *Why had he decided to buy the gun, anyway?* The rash of violent crime, not only on campus, but throughout the state, reported routinely every night on the television news, had made him feel unsafe. When Meredith was murdered he felt completely vulnerable, totally exposed, lacking any sense of protection. On one level, it was a compulsive purchase, a spontaneous reaction to a specific stimulus. Below that, however, was the deep seated need for security. Russell required something to satisfy that need, a need as basic as the one that caused a man first to lift a rock in response to a growl outside the mouth of his cave.

I ... **[Deleted]**
... – Home.
Emily Dickinson, from No. 190 Lines 3-4

12

Liz stood underneath the canopy, outside the remote door at the end of the industrial arts wing of the high school. Few students made use of this door, even fewer faculty members. She paced in circles on the small concrete pad.

Finally, Chris came around the corner of the building, checking over his shoulder.

"Chris!" she cried, rushing toward him, throwing her arms around his neck.

"Hey! Wha—" his words swallowed by Liz, her lips sealed around his mouth in a hungry grip.

"Whoa! What's this all about?" he asked, wrenching free to look down at her.

"You don't like?" she said, moving toward him again.

"Yeah, of course," he said, trying to maintain a distance as he looked around again. "What's going on?"

"I've missed you," she said, this time kissing him more gingerly.

"Yeah. Well, that's great. I miss you, too. But your text sounded urgent."

"It was urgent. I had to see you." Again she embraced him and began to kiss him more passionately.

"Not here! We'll both get detention."

Liz smiled at him, staring at his blue eyes, believing she could stare at them forever.

"What is it?" he asked.

"I can't stand it anymore. Let's get out of here, now."

"Now? I've got chemistry, now."

"Screw chemistry. Let's get in your car and go. I don't care where, just away from here. C'mon."

Chris looked at her, and she could sense his disbelief. She lifted the corners of her mouth in a small smile as she cocked her head.

"I know we're going to regret this," he said at last.

*When ...   **[Deleted]**   ... run –*
Emily Dickinson, from No. 156 Line 10

13

"You have some homework to do, Liz?" Michael asked. He placed his hand on Linda's wrist to urge her to sit back down. The dinner dishes could wait.

"No, I'm good," his daughter answered, not looking up from the screen of her cell phone.

"Go watch some TV, then."

She looked up at him now, and he returned a stern look to suggest he was serious.

"Okay," she groaned, and left the room displaying just enough teenage attitude.

Linda looked at him now. He could see that she was concerned.

"I got stopped today in Paterson," Michael began.

"By the cops?" Linda asked.

"No, worse. Two goons pulled in front of me in an alley near Rudy's. We had a little chat."

"What did they want?"

"They gave me an invitation." Michael handed Linda the address he had been given. After she unfolded it and read it, he continued. "Ironic, isn't it? I'm to meet them on Straight Street tomorrow night."

"What do they want?" she asked.

"They want to muscle in on the business. Take for free what I worked to put together."

"Mike, I don't like this."

"Me neither. But I'm sort of surprised it took

them this long. Independents don't seem to last long in this business." With his knife he began to draw a pattern in the sauce remaining in his dinner plate.

"What are you going to do?"

"I'll meet with them. Don't think I have much choice."

"No, it sounds too dangerous. I don't want you to get involved."

"Too late, Lin. They know who I am, probably know where we live."

Michael took her hands and felt a slight trembling. He gave them a reassuring squeeze. "I've thought about this," he continued. "As long as I play along, it's in their best interest to take care of me. If I defy them, well, that's when the harassment, the vandalism, whatever else, begins. And they know we can't go to the police."

"Then quit, Mike. I didn't like this idea from the beginning."

"That won't work, Lin. Liz starts college next fall. How we going to pay for that? Finding a job is next to impossible. You think we can make it on unemployment?"

"I hate this."

"I know, but the route pays so well because of the risks. You think Rudy likes working for hoodlums? All the legitimate businesses are gone now."

Desperation conquered the emotions on Linda's face. Michael could see it as her eyes grew dull, even as he felt that he was being sucked ever deeper into the abyss of a criminal life. Originally he had made such a small compromise, just a nod to the black market that suddenly appeared in response to the failure of the nation's economy. Now he felt his grip slipping, a loss of the control he had convinced himself he was maintaining.

"Oh, Mike, be careful!"

"I will, babe. I will."

From ...
[Deleted]
... hang!

Emily Dickinson, from No. 42 Lines 5-8

14

Russell scanned his email inbox, becoming excited when he spotted Karen's name in the list of senders. He sat forward in his chair to read it.

Hi Dad,
As you probably figured out by now, I'm in Israel, on business. The sales calls keep me busy; I'm visiting about seven locations each day. Don't worry though, the competition is pretty weak, and I'm sure I'll be able to close many deals without suffering any losses. There is nothing here as good as the product I'm selling. Will write again when I can. Love you and miss you,
Karen

Russell leaned back in his chair and chuckled. His daughter's encoded message was an effort to set his mind at ease. Still, it would take just a little bit of bad luck to bring her plane, and his world, crashing down.

He clicked the "reply" button and typed up a brief note, assuring her that all was well, that he prayed for her safety, that he loved and missed her, too.

All was well. There was a euphemism for you. Karen carried a .45, and for good reason. Why Russell carried an automatic pistol was not nearly as clear, although the feeling of invasion, of extreme encroachment, he felt after his wife's murder had compelled him to do so. Then there was the mysterious phone call, incredibly bizarre and strangely believable at the same time. Meanwhile, the economy continued to plummet, inflation and unemployment spiraled upward, as if the urgings of many prophets, including Meredith, were being purposely ignored so as to prove their points.

Rufus nudged him, reminding Russell that it was time for a walk. Russell smiled, the usual response to the dog's presence. Here, at least, in the relationship between man and canine, all was well.

> For ...   *[Deleted]*
> ... upon –
> Emily Dickinson, from No. 751 Lines 11-12

15

Jasper wheeled the Humvee sharply around the corner and behind the strip mall. Having to return to the armory to fill the gas tank had made them late for the rendezvous. A single lamp mounted on a pole behind the shopping center lit the five vehicles already assembled there and the men sitting on bumpers or leaning against hoods. Lt. Davis paced impatiently in front of them, and he turned and glared at Paul as he stepped out of his armored personnel carrier.

Lt. Davis was a tall man, and his arrow straight posture made him look taller. A dark-skinned African-American, the whites of his eyes were a marked contrast to the rest of his face, and accentuated the positioning of his rapidly shifting eyes, which paused long enough to appraise a situation before moving on to their next target. He had just a trace of a mustache which complemented the black stubble that ventured out from under his beret.

Once Jasper and Paul assumed standing positions near the edge of the group, Lt. Davis turned on his heel to face the group.

"Gentlemen, our target this evening is a meeting now convening at the Zion Lutheran Church. The subjects are believed to be right-wing reactionaries, generally hostile to the state. Although we have no intelligence that suggests that they are armed, you should use caution during every phase of this operation.

"Our mission is to create a perimeter around the building and contain all attendees of the meeting within the church. We will then enter the building, interrupt the proceedings, and then, in an organized fashion, record the names, addresses and Social Security numbers of all attendees. Afterwards, all present will be released to return to their homes. However, in the event there is any resistance or refusal to cooperate with our operation, anyone doing so will be arrested and transported to the Garfield Police headquarters for processing and formal charging. Are there any questions?"

Silence was the response. This, however, was interrupted by the crashing sound of a dumpster lid slamming closed. Lt. Davis turned his head toward the sound, and a teenager, wearing a white apron, sheepishly returned his stare, and then quickly walked back through the restaurant's back door.

Lt. Davis turned back to his men. "Stearns and Wiggins, you'll take the front door. Wolgamuth and Robinson, you'll take the rear. Perkins and Anderson, your responsibility is to record the identity information. You will examine official i.d. in each case. Anyone lacking official i.d., you bring to me. Hotchkiss and Zander, you will maintain perimeter security."

Davis scanned his men one last time. "Okay, let's saddle up."

* * * *

Paul spied the modest white steeple of Zion Lutheran Church as they approached on Midland Avenue. One of the bright red doors in the front of the church was open as they passed, and he got a glimpse of the crowd inside. The white clapboard walls loomed in the darkness. Light from inside made the blue stained glass windows glow. Red, white, and blue. Paul sensed the irony immediately.

"This doesn't seem right," Paul said to Jasper as the Humvee slipped into the church parking lot with its headlights extinguished. "This is a church, for crying out loud."

"That's probably what they were thinking," Jasper volunteered. "'No one will bother us in a church.'"

"And why should anyone bother them? This is still America, isn't it?"

"I'm sure Lt. Davis wouldn't send us here if the intel wasn't good. We better get in position."

A few minutes later, Paul was quietly treading through the leaves in the rear churchyard and climbing the steps to the back door, Jasper following close behind.

Through the earplug in his left ear he heard Sterno's voice. "Swish, you in position?"

"Roger that," Paul whispered into his radio.

"Let's do it."

Paul flicked on the flashlight mounted on his M16 and tugged open the door. He swept the light quickly around the darkened antechamber and moved quickly towards the light and voices coming from the sanctuary. He heard a sudden change in the sounds from the room and knew that the occupants were aware of Sterno and Hairdo entering the hall. Just as Paul reached the doorway, he faced a thin bald man wearing glasses attempting to exit. Paul barred the door with his rifle and swung it like a gate to direct the man back inside. The voices were now louder and more excited.

He looked into the room from a door off the raised altar. The interior was wood-paneled with red carpeting, which gave the church a warm, modest, utilitarian feel. The hundred or so occupants were a good fit. Everyday attire predominated. The men wore sports shirts and hunting jackets rather than suits and ties, the women more often had on sweaters and pants than dresses. Most were standing among the pews, obviously surprised and confused. At the front door he saw Hairdo and Sterno, the latter with a hand in the air and raising his voice above the crowd's voices. "Everyone remain calm. There is no need for alarm."

The bald man stood a few feet away, as if waiting for an opportunity to slip past Paul and out the back door. A woman and two men were climbing the stairs behind him. Paul stepped forward to turn the bald man around and abort the other's climb.

"What's going on?" asked the bald man.

Paul assumed his most official sounding voice. "Please, just return to your seat."

"I demand to know what's going on," the bald man pressed.

"Please. Return to your seat," Paul countered. "Everything will be explained."

The bald man glared at Paul as he turned towards the stairs.

At the front door, Paul saw Lt. Davis enter behind Sterno. He was accompanied by a middle aged man, dressed in a suit and black overcoat. Davis and his well dressed companion moved along the wall toward the altar, the lieutenant shaking off the numerous supplications he encountered along the way. The civilian escaped such attention, the meeting's attendees mistakenly assigning more authority to the man in uniform.

When they reached the pulpit, Davis stepped to the microphone and tapped it gently, the thuds amplified into the church. Apparently the chairman of the meeting had stood there, and Davis scooped up a clutch of papers off the lectern and handed them to Perkins, who had made entry without Paul seeing him. With a quick glance back to the front door Paul saw Anderson setting up a card table as Hairdo guarded the exit.

Davis's crisp, strong voice probably needed

no microphone, but with the amplification it sounded more authoritative. "In accordance with Executive Order 2177, a Declaration of Martial Law, these proceedings are judged to be outside the parameters of a peaceable assembly, in that they suggest, advocate, endorse, or otherwise encourage the overthrow of the Government of the United States or to hinder the proper functioning of said government. As such, any one in attendance at this meeting is subject to arrest and the filing of criminal charges for violating this Executive Order."

The crowd became vocal with this pronouncement. Most spoke among themselves, a look of bewildered concern common on their faces. A few shouted protests towards the pulpit.

Davis's voice became even more commanding as he attempted to speak over the crowd. "However…" He paused to allow them to calm down. "However…" Davis took up a gavel and brought it down forcefully three times on the lectern, its ringing amplification working to nearly silence the audience. "However, it is not our intent to make any arrests this evening. Instead, I ask for your cooperation. We will dismiss each pew, in turn. When dismissed, please have your photo identification out and present it to Private Anderson seated at the table near the front door. Once he has recorded your information, you will be free to leave the church and return to your homes. Do not linger in the churchyard or in the parking lot. Do not speak to anyone as you leave. We have guardsmen outside to insure these instructions are followed."

Davis turned to look at the man in the suit, who nodded back silently.

"The rear pew on the left, you are dismissed," Davis called as he pointed in that direction.

The crowd again became talkative. Paul watched their faces. He could see their confusion. He could sense how alien such a forceful military presence was in their lives. He had no trouble understanding their anguish, for he felt it too.

Suddenly, above the noise of the crowd, Paul could hear one voice, louder and clearer than the others. Though not amplified, he sounded nearly as loud as Davis had. Paul spotted him. He was a rotund man, his small head sitting like a small cherry atop a huge scoop of ice cream in a sundae. He had disheveled, greasy black hair and wore a white shirt with the sleeves rolled up on his forearms. With his right index finger he punctuated each word that he addressed towards Lt. Davis, still standing at the pulpit. Bursts of saliva that shot from his mouth added additional emphasis. "This violates our Constitutional right to peaceably assemble. This right is guaranteed in the First Amendment to the Constitution. 'Congress shall make no law respecting an establishment of religion, or prohibiting the free exercise thereof; or abridging the freedom of speech, or of the press, or the right of the people—'"

Jasper had grabbed the man by the collar and yanked him into the center aisle. Clutching at successive pews to slow his extrication, the man was no match for Jasper's strength. In a moment he was being dragged up the steps and past Paul, who stepped aside to allow them to exit the door behind him. Paul stepped in the opposite direction to allow Perkins to pass and join Jasper. Paul remained in position and continued to scan the crowd. While their protests became angrier and their faces more concerned, their voices became more subdued. The arrest of the large man served to temper their displays, as removing a kettle from the flame quells the rolling boil but not its contents' potential to scald.

And in that uneasy calm, Paul again felt tugs of doubt on his heart. He doubted that this gathering of typical, apparently law-abiding citizens was a threat to anyone, and particularly to a properly constituted and appropriately functioning government. He suddenly felt unclean, as if the camo uniform was secreting a slimy ooze onto his skin. The helmet on his head took on added weight, and suddenly, it felt like it might pinch his head right off his neck and then fall to cap and disguise what it had done. His boots, too, felt heavy, anchoring him to the floor. The rifle strap dug into his neck, as if to aid the helmet in its plan for decapitation. Paul raised the rifle slightly to ease the strain. Once more he checked to be sure the safety was on.

> The ...   *[Deleted]*
> ... *done*
> Emily Dickinson, from No. 1293 Lines 1-2

16

Linda turned in response to the soft knock on the classroom door. She stepped to the door where a girl handed her a note, folded in two. It was a phone message form, asking her to call back Mr. Barnes from Garfield High School, and providing a phone number. Linda thanked the messenger, probably a freshman since Linda did not know her by name, and slipped the note into a pocket as she returned to her lecture. Why would Liz's school need to talk to her?

Her efforts for the remainder of the period were ineffective. She could not remain focused, the nature of the phone call like a weight on her mind. She stumbled through her lecture, which became disjointed. She wasn't truly listening to students' responses, and once she actually had to ask the student to repeat her answer. At last the bell rang. From the relative privacy of the teachers' lounge, Linda dialed Garfield High. Mr. Barnes, the Assistant Principal, wasted no time getting to the point.

"It seems your daughter left the high school campus yesterday afternoon, missing two of her classes."

"Liz? She cut class?"

"Yes. We confronted her, and she admits that she and Chris Martin, as she put it, 'took the afternoon off.'"

"What?"

"Yes, we were a little surprised, too. Liz is an honor roll student, and this is not typical behavior for her. It's not typical of Mr. Martin, either, so, naturally we were concerned. We're obligated to apprise you of the situation."

"Yes, of course. What disciplinary action are you taking?"

"Given their clean records, we have decided to impose an academic probation. Another serious infraction could result in suspension, possibly jeopardize graduation. You should appreciate that we are being lenient here, but we cannot tolerate this behavior continuing."

"Yes, I understand. Thank you, Mr. Barnes. I can assure you we will talk to Liz this evening when she gets home from work."

Over ...   **[Deleted]**
           ... – again!
           Emily Dickinson, from No. 156 Lines 18-19

17

"Good afternoon, Mr. Grayson." The voice was deep, self-assured, and Russell recognized it immediately. He set aside the Emily Dickinson volume he had been reading.

"Why, hello…I'm not sure how I should address you," Russell responded.

"There is no need; I do not exist. The sooner you remember that, the safer we both will be."

"Right."

"Have you thought about what we talked about before?"

"The subject matter was…compelling. Yes, I've thought of it often."

"And?"

"And I'm not really sure how to proceed—what you're expecting of me."

"Let me change my approach, then. I'll give you some information. You're a smart guy, a professor, no less. You'll be able to figure out what to do. You ready?"

"Yes," Russell said as he took a pen from his pocket.

"Okay, the subject of interest is Alberto Gonzalez, born, raised and still residing in Paterson. Got that?"

"Yes—"

The line went dead. Russell exhaled audibly, and stared at the three words scribbled on his notepad. The names went blurry as tears filled his eyes. There, in his hands, was the name of the man that most likely had murdered Meredith. This was information that he had fervently hoped to know, and always had assumed he would learn only after an arrest, if ever. Suddenly, he didn't feel all that smart.

* * * *

"Hey, Win!" Russell called, as the professor strode away down the hall. Her long legs threatened to take her around the corner and out of sight before Russell could catch up.

"Hi, Russ," she said, stopping to await his approach. "What brings you to the commercial corridors of the College of Business?"

Russell smiled. Winifred McDonald never hesitated to employ self-effacing language when speaking of the business college in the presence of the liberal arts faculty. She was no slouch as a writer, though. Russell had admired all of her books for their clear and accessible style. She had been Meredith's close friend, and had accompanied them on weekend jaunts.

"Just a quick favor," he said. "I remember you speaking of a private investigator that helped you with your divorce. Could I get his contact information?"

"Jeff? Wow, that was a few years ago, and I know he was talking about packing it in back then. You need someone investigated?"

"Sort of." Russell answered, while averting his eyes to the floor. "What was his last name, again? Maybe I can track him down."

"It was 'Downs,'" she said. "Call my attorney, Barry Silverstein. He's in Springfield. I'm sure he can help you."

"Thanks, Win."

"Any time." She moved slightly closer and adopted a more confidential tone. "How are you doing?"

"I'm doing okay…all things considered."

"We should have dinner sometime. You look like you're losing weight."

"Yeah. Yeah, we should. That's a good idea."

"If I can do anything for you, you know to call, right?"

"You just did. Thanks, Win."

The ...
 [Deleted]
  ... death –
  Emily Dickinson, from No. 762 Lines 5-8

18

The bus squealed and squeaked to a halt, letting out a hiss as the door opened. Liz bounded down the steps into the night, waiting on the shoulder to let the bus proceed on its way before she crossed the road. It was only a short walk to her house, a fact that had made commuting by bus to her part-time job such a viable option. She walked along the shoulder of the roadway, as there was no sidewalk. Her feet rustled through the leaves that already had fallen and had been swept to the roadside by the wind and passing traffic.

She felt a pang of hunger, the pizza slice she had eaten hours ago now almost forgotten. Accompanying that sensation was a twist to her stomach in the opposite direction—the realization that a paper was due tomorrow, and she hadn't begun to work on it. It was a quarter to nine, and a long night loomed ahead.

She sensed it before she opened the door to the house, a feeling of uneasiness. This feeling intensified as she entered the kitchen to find both her parents seated at the kitchen table. A sinking feeling overcame her. *This could not be good.*

"Hi," she said, attempting an air of normalcy.

"Come sit down, Liz," said her father. *Not a good sign.*

"What's up?" she asked, feigning ignorance. She wasn't sure why she bothered, clearly the inquisition was about to begin.

"I got a call from Mr. Barnes, today," her mother began.

"Oh, about that. I can explain." *Quickly now, she had to get her head in the game.*

"Explain that you cut two classes? How can you explain that?"

"Mom, I just needed a break. The pressure was like, intense. I had to get out of there for an hour or two. It's never happened before; it won't happen again. I promise."

"And Christopher needed a break, too?" her father chimed in. *Two against one, this wasn't fair.*

"Yeah, well, Chris and me, we talked. It helped a lot. Later, I was much better."

"Liz, when Chris tried to get you to cut, you should have been stronger. You should have told him 'no,'" her mother said. *She almost sounded sympathetic.*

"Chris didn't ask me," Liz confessed. "I asked him. It was all my idea."

"What? That makes it even worse," her father remarked. *He didn't sound sympathetic at all.*

"Liz, honey, this isn't like you. We've come to expect you to make mature decisions. Now, in your last year of high school, you pull this? Don't you understand the possible consequences?" *Typical Mom, like she was teaching from a lesson plan. Everything thought out and logical. So unrealistic.*

"I'm sorry. Like I said, I wasn't thinking. The stress was just too much and I panicked."

"It affects more than just you," said her father. "Now you admit you dragged Christopher into this. And both of your reputations might suffer as a result." *Typical Dad, the Drama King.*

"Dad, it's 'Chris.' He hates to be called 'Christopher.'"

"I don't care what his name is. Both of you showed poor judgment. I'm beginning to wonder if he might be a bad influence on you."

"I told you, I influenced him. I'm responsible. Don't blame Chris."

"Well, I think you're seeing too much of him," her father continued.

"No! Don't say that. I love Chris." *Blurting that out was not the best plan. Maybe she could backtrack a little.* "I mean—" she paused to regroup. "Chris is a good friend. We're good for each other."

The room fell silent. Liz's eyes joined her mother's to focus on her father. *Mom was deferring to him. That was not a positive sign.*

"I can't tell you how disappointed I am," her father began. "This stunt could have gotten you suspended. As it is, you're on scholastic probation. You must realize how serious we are about this. I don't want you to see Chris any more. Even at school, I don't want you seeing him—only what you must do because of class. No more phone or internet contact. Not until we are convinced you can act in a responsible manner again. Do you understand me?"

Liz's heart dropped into her stomach even as tears rose in her eyes. *This was unfair. He had no idea how much this hurt her.* But experience had taught her she had no hope of changing his mind.

"Yes," she said, trying to hold back her tears.

I'm ...
[Deleted]
... us!

Emily Dickinson, from No. 288 Lines 1-3

19

Russell pulled into Jeff Down's driveway. The house was a small ranch, surrounded by well-tended flower gardens that stretched from the curb to the house's foundation. Even this late in the fall, the gardens were abloom with chrysanthemums of various colors. It had taken him most of an hour to drive down here, and he found the beautiful, quiet gardens to be welcoming.

The door was opened by a striking woman, whose long dark hair was tied in a long pony tail that wrapped around her neck.

"You must be Mr. Grayson," she said. "Please come in, and I'll get Jeff."

Russell took a seat in the compact living room, the simple furnishings made more attractive as they were surrounded by a profusion of robust house plants. In no time, the woman returned, followed by a broad-shouldered man who walked with a pronounced limp. He shook Russell's hand and motioned for him to sit.

"Thanks, Dolores," he said, and he turned to watch her leave the room. Once she left, he turned back to Russell. "So, Professor Grayson, I am intrigued by your determination to seek out this old, broken down, retired p.i. Let me say it again, for emphasis: 'retired'."

"Thank you for agreeing to see me. Winifred

McDonald speaks very highly of you."

"How is Winnie? A most remarkable woman, and an interesting case for me, too."

The detective presented many contradictions, insisting that he was retired but receptive to a meeting; presenting a rough and tumble physique, but speaking with a glint in his eye that suggested a playful, insightful mind.

"Win is well. She just finished a book on management flaws and their consequences. It sounds like a dry topic, but the book is a page-turner."

"That's good to hear. But what brings you to me? Would I be wrong in guessing it has something to do with the tragic death of your wife? My condolences regarding that, by the way."

"Why, thank you. I'm surprised you knew."

"To be a good detective, you have to be inquisitive. One man's inquisitiveness is another's nosiness, I'm afraid. Your phone call got me to asking questions, and the internet provided some answers. It didn't take long to find the link between you and Landers' economic advisor. I guessed you must be interested in the murders."

"Your research is right on. Saves me telling a great deal of background, too."

"So how do you think I can help you solve a multiple murder in Fort Wayne? I confess to being inquisitive, but not clairvoyant."

Russell described the phone calls, as best he could recall, and in detail, and responded to Downs' occasional questions.

"Sounds like your 'Deep Throat' is an investigator on the inside," Downs concluded. "Probably scared shitless to tell you even what he did. What motivates him could be anybody's guess—fear of the investigation collapsing around him, some kind of beef with a higher-up that he'd like to settle in an embarrassing way, or maybe he's still a 'boy scout,' who still believes in Truth, Justice and the American

Way."

"Do you think there's a cover up going on?" Russell asked.

"Could be. Two months is a long time without a collar in a case like this. Either the perps are very good, or..."

"Or?"

"Or, sorry professor, but perhaps they aren't supposed to get caught." Downs said.

Downs resumed the conversation, perhaps to lessen the pain. "What was the name he gave you?" he asked.

"Alberto Gonzalez. Of Paterson."

"Once a jewel on the Passaic River," Downs volunteered. "now, much of it a cesspool."

Downs sat quietly, his eyes closed, an index finger resting on the bridge of his nose, the tip pressing between his eyebrows. Russell was uncertain whether he was thinking or had dozed off. At last the detective spoke.

"I'll look into it for you. I've got some contacts in the Paterson P.D. Used to be a cop myself, in Jersey City. I worked there until—" Downs pointed to his lame leg, "until I took disability. Let me see what I can turn up, and we'll go from there."

"Thank you, Mr. Downs."

"Jeff. Call me 'Jeff.'"

Our ...   ***[Deleted]***
         ... shy –

Emily Dickinson, from No. 274 Lines 13-14

20

Michael pulled his car to the curb and shut off the headlights. This part of Paterson seemed uninhabited, and the overcast skies prevented moonlight from descending. To his left, across an empty parking lot, was the high concrete wall that supported the railroad tracks through the city center. To his right, a plumbing and heating dealership was dark, its day-time occupants long departed with the setting sun. Michael felt terribly alone.

He took the paper from his pocket and by the light from his car's dome light, confirmed the address painted on the white bricks of the plumbing store. He glanced at his watch to check the time.

He stepped from the car and looked around before walking to the door. The knob remained immobile, the door secure. Locked up tight.

Michael started back to his car, but before he reached the door, headlights came up the street and a dark sedan stopped before him. He recognized the front-seat passenger as Marv.

"Follow us, Michael."

Michael followed the car as it zigzagged through the city's grid, pulling at last into the empty parking lot of an elementary school. Michael imagined what the school playground was like during the day, filled with energetic kids. Now, it was dark and eerie, a single mercury vapor lamp illuminating the far corner. Michael pulled up next to Marv's window.

"Park here and join us."

Michael slid into the back seat. The car reeked of cigarette smoke. The stocky fellow was driving tonight, but made no effort to greet his new passenger. They drove on in silence, through a residential neighborhood. Here and there a porch light burned, but for the most part the inhabitants had retreated within their homes. Their presence was revealed sometimes by an illuminated reading lamp visible through a window, more often by the flickering bluish glow from a television. The car's frequent turns soon disoriented Michael so he had no idea where they were within the city's matrix.

They pulled behind a non-descript frame house and parked in the alley. Michael followed Marv up the back steps and the stocky fellow followed him. Passing through a spartan kitchen, they entered a sitting room, where three men were sharing a spacious couch.

Understatement was the theme of the house. Modest furnishings, simple designs, limited, almost motel-style artwork—all these suggested the house only had a utilitarian purpose. It all said about whoever lived here that they had to, not that they wanted to.

The thin man on the left was wedged in the corner of the couch, a leg thrown over a knee, sitting as if he were nursing a severe case of inflamed hemorrhoids. His narrow face suggested that at any minute he might cry out in pain. From behind thick lenses, his eyes sized Michael up from top to bottom.

As thin as the man on the left was, obesity was the claim of his counterpart on the right. His long-sleeve shirt was open at the collar, and a paisley tie hung loosely around his neck. Both feet were on the floor, knees spread wide, so that the mass of his gut was prominently displayed. Few hairs adorned his head, and his forehead was moist with perspiration, although Michael found the room temperature not unusually warm.

In the center sat a casually dressed man, a few years younger than his companions. His powder blue polo shirt did little to conceal the muscular nature of his shoulders. His tanned skin contrasted with the light colored fabric, which fit tight enough to suggest rippled abdomen muscles beneath it. His hair was brown, as was the thin mustache just above his lip. Dark brown eyes studied Michael as he entered the room and stood before a glass coffee table that separated him from the men on the couch.

"Mr. Norton, please sit down," said the man in the center, motioning to a chair behind Michael. "You want a cup of coffee? Or a beer, maybe?"

"No, thanks," Michael responded, seating himself.

"I want to thank you for joining us this evening," the man said. My colleagues and I have an exciting proposition we want to discuss with you."

"Uh huh," Michael said cautiously, crossing his arms over his chest. Then, thinking that position too defensive, he repositioned his arms to the armrests of the chair.

"I am Alberto," the man said, nodding forward slightly.

"Just 'Alberto'?"

"Yes, just 'Alberto'. It is enough. May I call you 'Michael'?"

"Yeah, sure."

"Okay, then. Michael, my associates and I have been impressed with the business you got going in a very short time. We want to give you a chance to expand your business, while at the same time giving you protection from the risks and dangers you might face."

"And what's this going to cost me?"

"Now, Michael, it sounds like you see the costs without considering the benefits. When you weigh the two together, you'll find the benefits far outweigh the minimal cost."

"Really?" Michael again found his arms crossed over his chest, then moved his hands down to his waist. Reconsidering his posture and the message it might send, he returned his hands to the armrests.

"Absolutely. For example, your operation runs—how do I say this?—slightly contrary to the laws of the State of New Jersey. Could you imagine a time when it might be a good idea to have someone intercede in your behalf? A state official who is sympathetic to the difficulties you face as an independent business man? Yes? Well, we have access to such officials—at high levels. Why, just one time such as this could be very costly to you—impoundment of your truck, fines, jail time. It could put you out of business in one swoop. On the other hand, an official, sympathetic to our business interests, could make the complaint fall into some bureaucratic black hole and—POOF!—problem solved. Do you see what I mean?"

"Sure."

A loud hiss erupted over Michael's shoulder. He spun his head around to see the heavy man who had driven him here sucking the foam off the top of a can of beer he had just opened. He looked up sheepishly at the looks of admonishment sent his way from the men on the couch, but said nothing as he stepped backwards a few steps and began to drink.

"Okay, then. That's one example. Here's another: suppose somebody—some mobster, gang member, whatever—suppose he messes with your truck. You know, slashes your tires, puts sugar in your fuel tank, torches your cab—the possibilities are endless." Alberto leaned forward, as if to bring Michael into his confidence. "Well, first of all, once you join us, the word gets around pretty fast. Many of the criminal element know not to screw with us. That alone is a big benefit. But should somebody be fool enough as to attack you or your truck—well, let me just say, they'll regret that decision. You understand?"

"Right." Michael had heard that Alberto had used vandalism to pressure drivers into joining his syndicate. Michael was tempted to ask Alberto if he used such tactics on his own drivers, but thought better of it.

"So what do you think? Could you use such protection?"

"I'm sitting here thinking," Michael responded, "why me? Why, of all the truck drivers in New Jersey, you choose to invite me into your little… club?"

"Like I said, we are impressed with your business sense. You built a route quickly. And we noticed that you picked up mostly the fancier restaurants. We bet your sales margins are higher than average because of that. We're looking for somebody with that kind of smarts to join us and help us grow."

Michael wondered how they knew this. They must have been following him for several days. "All right, suppose I choose to join you. What's it going to cost me?"

"These are difficult times, Michael. We understand that. We do everything we can to make it affordable." Alberto sat back on the sofa, and nodded to the small man to his right.

Taking his cue, the thin man sat even more erect in his corner. "Our fee is eight per cent of your gross," he said. "Our week runs Sunday through Saturday. Your fee is due to us on the morning of the following Monday."

Michael was not surprised by the figure. Talking with other drivers, who had been careful in revealing these details, Michael knew what to expect going in. He had also learned that in a rare demonstration of compassion, the rate had dropped from ten per cent two years into the latest economic downturn.

The huge man on the right chimed in without prompting. "Don't even *think* about running part of your operation 'off the books.' That would be a big mistake. If we find out—and we usually do—you could lose your membership."

"Please pardon Sam's directness," Alberto said, leaning forward again, "but we've had some problems in the past, and we just like to get a clear understanding from the beginning."

"Uh huh," Michael acknowledged.

"You have any questions?"

Michael had many questions, but few for Alberto. He questioned how successful he would be marking up his meat prices to help cover the cut for his new "partners." He wondered how he could continue to grow the business, since most of his success had been due to his ability, as an independent contractor, to undercut the competition that was "affiliated" with various crime organizations. Mostly, Michael questioned if he would ever be able to reverse this plunge deeper into the underworld. How many of the associations he would soon be making would follow him, and haunt him, should the economic conditions improve and he tried again to become legitimate?

One thing was not in question: he had no choice but to accept Alberto's offer. They had his number. He had few alternatives. The word on the street was that Alberto was not one to disappoint.

> *I'm ...*   ***[Deleted]***
>   *... be –*
>
>   Emily Dickinson, from No. 256 Lines 10-11

21

"Grounded! For three weeks!" Chris collapsed against a nearby locker with the clanking sound made by every student who slammed his locker door. The cacophony was such that it made the hallways during the short time between classes sound like a steel stamping factory. His eyes were closed as his head rested against the locker, his face to the ceiling.

"Yeah, my parents freaked, too," Liz said, as she swapped her psychology text for her biology book on the floor of her locker. "I'm banned from seeing you, except in classes."

"Great. I knew cutting was a bad idea." Chris kept his eyes closed as he brought his fists down to thump the locker again.

"You didn't have a good time?" Liz asked, hanging onto the locker door and looking up at Chris from beneath arched eyebrows.

Chris looked down at her and smiled. "Of course, I did. But it cost me. My dad took my car keys, and now I've got to ride the stupid school bus. They won't even let me ride to school with Kevin! This sucks!"

Liz grabbed his hand and gave it a squeeze. "Well, I'm glad you came with me. You were there for me when I needed you."

Chris smiled back. "I always want to be there for you, Liz. I gotta get to math."

"Okay, I'll see you later."

A quick kiss, and then he was lost in the passing flow of students.

Liz closed her locker and sighed. She felt very much alone, with her one true friend now available to her only in clandestine meetings. Life was suddenly becoming complicated, and the biology test next period wasn't helping.

For each ecstatic instant
We must an anguish pay
                        Emily Dickinson, from No. 125

22

Linda collapsed upon Michael, her dead weight completely drained of the energy it possessed just minutes before. She was no burden on him—quite the opposite. She was his strength and his support.

He had initiated tonight's lovemaking, with nothing more than a few gentle strokes on her back. She had responded, quietly, aggressively—despite how tired she must have been—as if she knew how helpless he felt and how important it was that he knew he could still seduce her.

The meeting with Alberto was their new crisis. It had dominated their conversation, at least whenever Liz was out of earshot. Michael could see that Linda was worried. "A deal with the devil" she had called it, and he could not argue. The new partnership was not his choice, nor would he have chosen Alberto and his friends for any role in his life.

He felt he was losing control of his business, of his livelihood, of his life. It seemed that more and more of the decisions he was making were beyond his control. This fired anger within him, but he could not vent the flames in any of the directions he wished. This, too, was a choice outside of his control.

He was rather proud of himself, actually. He had been able to keep his anger under control. Close calls on the highways—far from uncommon—no longer caused him to swear or vent at the other drivers. As if the new threats to his livelihood had muscled aside less significant concerns, his focus on his job—doing it safely, inconspicuously—was now paramount. He was less inclined to rush to his next delivery, but would drop his speed five miles below the posted limit. No need to invite Johnny Law into his life. Even a minor traffic accident could be devastating if a traffic cop got the wrong feeling about him or his cargo. Black markets were popping up everywhere, but they were still illegal. Some gung-ho Super Trooper could really mess things up further. He had to protect what mattered most. What mattered most was all he had left.

That was Linda and Liz. Liz was growing up fast and was already beginning to cut tethers. This was expected, and he could live with her new maturity.

Linda, however, was different. Yes, she was loving. She proved it again tonight. She could have said, "Not tonight," and he would have understood. He would not have pressed the issue. Instead, she had consented, and been an energetic participant: enticing, accepting, surrendering, and coaxing. And when, once again, he proved to be unequal to the task, she had neither questioned nor condemned, but acted as if everything was as it should be. Whether from sheer exhaustion or sincere concern for his feelings, she had collapsed onto his chest and into his possessive arms. For reasons he couldn't explain, she was loyal to him. He would strive to deserve that devotion.

Quickly she fell asleep, and he lay there, feeling her gentle breaths and occasional involuntary flinches. He held her. Tightly. But the more he squeezed, the less he contained.

Grabbing the remote off the nightstand, he flipped on the television, muting the sound. CNN was showing videotape coverage of the riots in Newark. Michael was not alone in his desperation, as he watched flat screen televisions in shopping carts being rolled out of looted department stores and apartment houses going up in smoke. He wasn't *that* desperate! He couldn't imagine torching his own neighborhood or looting the local market. How far can a man be pushed by forces outside his control? How much more was he capable of withstanding?

Surgeons must be very careful
When they take the knife!
Emily Dickinson, from No. 108

23

"Focus your eyes on the front sight," Lance said. "The target should appear a little fuzzy, out of focus."

Russell did as instructed, and the bulls-eye target at the end of the dimly lit shooting range went soft. Not focusing his eyes on the target—that was the first non-intuitive thing Lance had suggested. "Focus on the goal" had always been the cliché. When it got down to it, it proved to be inaccurate.

Earlier the firearms instructor, hired by the hour to make Russell a competent shooter, had given predictable, common sense comments as he discussed gun safety and care for the weapon. Now they had moved to the range, choosing lane number three, a narrow corridor of emptiness, with a paper target mounted on a motorized caddy at one end, and at the other, a small cubicle isolating the lane from #2 and #4.

"Now, align the front sight so that it fills the gap between the risers of the rear sight. Just like I showed you inside. The top of the rear sight should be level with the front sight."

"Got it," Russell said.

"Okay, rest the target on top of the rear sight, still maintaining the alignment and the levelness."

"Okay," Russell affirmed.

"Good, squeeze the trigger."

The explosion was loud. Even with the ear protectors, it was a piercing sound, and Russell jumped slightly. The recoil raced up his forearms and bounced off his elbows. The sound echoed around the chamber, and before it completed its rounds, he heard the tiny tinkle of the expelled brass hitting the concrete floor. The smell of gunpowder was an intoxicating scent.

Russell looked downrange at the target and spotted the small dark hole in the white paper to the right of the bulls-eye.

"Looks like you didn't squeeze the trigger, but pulled it. It's a common mistake of first-time shooters." Lance pointed his unloaded weapon downrange. "Watch. When I *pull* the trigger, see how the barrel is pulled to the right? When you *squeeze*, like this, you maintain the alignment. Look where my finger makes contact with the trigger. Everything must be controlled."

"Okay," Russell said.

"Try it again."

Russell again took aim, and made a conscious effort to squeeze the trigger. The report and recoil were expected this time, and he heard the spent shell casing more clearly when it hit the floor. Looking at the target, he was pleased to see a new hole, in the lower right quadrant of the black bulls-eye.

"Much better," Lance said. "You gettin' the feel for it?"

"I think so," Russell cautiously answered.

Where ...   ***[Deleted]***   *... tread –*
Emily Dickinson, from No. 104 Line 1

24

He spotted them after his third delivery. Stopped at a traffic light on Kinderkamack Road, Michael checked his rear-view mirror and saw the dark sedan about five cars back. Ever since his meeting with Alberto and his people, Michael had been more concerned about being followed. Although it had been fully expected, he still found it disconcerting.

Michael had come to terms with the taking of his money. He had rationalized it along the same lines that Alberto's accountant had laid out. The intrusion into his life, however, was a different matter. Clearly Alberto's boys had been snooping around before the meeting, and that activity would only intensify as the relationship between Michael and Alberto's organization developed. Michael resented that Alberto's men could show up anytime, anywhere, without notice. Like an insect in a pitcher plant, Michael felt like he was being drawn, irreversibly, inevitably into the sweet smelling goo that would result in his death.

The light changed, and Michael turned right, off the direct course to his next customer. He watched his mirror to see the sedan turn as well, slowing to maintain a discreet distance. Abruptly, Michael turned right again, into a residential neighborhood, and accelerated down the street. In the mirror he could see the sedan hesitate at the intersection, and then continue straight ahead, not turning to follow him.

Another right turn and Michael was headed back towards Kinderkamack Road. He had shaken them rather easily, but he knew they'd be back. His boxy white truck was easy to spot, especially behind many of Bergen County's finer restaurants.

* * * *

Michael stopped for lunch at a luncheonette in Oradell. He had taken one bite of his egg salad sandwich when Marv and his rotund companion came in, taking seats on either side of him at the counter.

"Care to join me?" Michael asked, after they were seated.

Marv did not look amused. "That was a cute stunt you pulled earlier," he said. "You're not helping yourself or Alberto by making our job more difficult."

Michael turned to Marv's partner. "I don't believe we've been introduced. I'm Michael Norton," he said, offering his hand.

The large man continued to look ahead and said nothing. Marv's voice became more serious, if that were possible. "This is not a game, Michael. You've got a job to do, and so do we. Let's all do it easily and efficiently."

Michael turned to Marv and looked him directly in the eyes. He had seen more compassion in the eyes of cobras at the zoo. "Look," he said, "I'm just used to having a little more personal space. It freaks me out to have you two mutts show up without warning. It's not that I'm anti-social, just…independent."

"Get over it, Michael. Your independent days are over. It's a new world now; the rules have changed. Survival is not as easy as it used to be. If you want to make it, you'd better get used to the new rules."

Michael turned away and glanced up at the

television, playing muted at the end of the counter. On the screen, APC's filled with National Guard troops were arriving in Newark.

Feet, ...   ***[Deleted]***
                  ... Drum –
            Emily Dickinson, from No. 295 Lines 17-18

25

"Over there!" Paul said to Jasper, pointing toward the old department store that fronted on Broad Street. The big man wheeled the Humvee to the left, sweeping through a large curve in the intersection. Few vehicles were on the streets, but people were everywhere, spilling off the sidewalks to cross the streets in all directions or ripple down them in small streams. Those in the street made way for the military vehicle, though reluctantly, as if it were an intruder and this, their daily routine. Few were empty-handed, many were hefting all that they could possibly carry—a large corrugated box, or several small cartons bearing illustrations identifying their contents as small household appliances or electronic components. Here and there a large television was carried away. A half-dozen young men and women loaded the bed of a pickup truck pulled to the curb on Market Street just east of Broad.

People were streaming out of the store through the window displays, powdering beneath their feet the glass which had been the windows. Some carried appliances, others had garments draped over their shoulders, while still others carried large shopping bags filled with merchandise not easily defined. Most of the looters were black, although Latinos were in abundance, too. Here and there were some white faces, while a group of Central Asians were identifiable by the head scarves on the women, scrupulously maintaining their chastity as they violated the Eighth Commandment.

The two men hopped out of the vehicle, Jasper taking the keys with him. Sterno and Hairdo pulled up immediately behind them in their own armored vehicle. The four soldiers moved towards the store front, just as two citizens attempted to extricate a large gas grill over the trampled window display and through the window opening onto the sidewalk.

"You're busted!" shouted Hairdo as he grabbed the man outside the window by his shirt collar, causing him to lose his grip on the grill which fell to the ground with a metallic bang.

Paul lunged through the window and grabbed the belt of the accomplice, who was attempting to retreat into the store. "Not so fast, Bucko!" Paul shouted.

"Get off me, man!" the thief shrieked, squirming to get free.

Sterno's hand joined Paul's on the looter's belt. The two pulled the man onto the sidewalk, each using one hand, their right hands grasping the weapons that were slung over their necks. "Lie on the ground and put your hands behind your head!" Paul instructed.

"We weren't doin' nothin'" said the larger rioter, who had already found his way to the ground through the courtesy of having his own feet displaced by a sweep of Jasper's large foot.

"Yeah, yeah, tell it to the judge," Jasper said.

Sterno was busy binding the hands of the criminals using plastic ties, when two other passersby attempted to lift the grill.

"Hey!!" Paul shouted. "You got 'im, Dennis?"
"Yeah, I'm good."

Paul wheeled and confronted the new contestants. The one closest to him turned simultaneously, dropping the grill for a second time. Paul looked up to see a jet black pistol leveled at him. Later he would tell how the threat had never really registered in his mind nor had he thought about what happened next. It was all an automatic reaction. Paul whipped his rifle around, the barrel striking the handgun and knocking it into the air. The rifle's strap jerked at Paul's neck, and in response he spun around a full clock-wise spin, forcefully landing the butt of his weapon against the looter's jaw. The man dropped to his knees, stunned. Paul re-directed the recoil of his flailing rifle back toward the man, the butt striking him again, opening a three inch gash in his forehead. Again, the butt came downward, striking the man in the jaw with a crunching sound. Paul pivoted his weapon and thrust the barrel at the looter's solar plexus, forcing him to double over and to fall back down against his heels. The man's partner had seen enough, and fled south on Broad Street.

Sterno constrained Paul with his left arm and pulled him away before he inflicted more damage, scooping up the pistol off the sidewalk in the same motion. "Whoa, there, Swish!" he cried, "He's down! He's down!"

Paul looked on as if he were a bystander, his own confusion matched by the dazed look the looter returned his way from the sidewalk. Paul had had his first taste of combat, and had come out on top. He felt good about that outcome, but he was not at all comfortable with the beast that had been released.

By ...
   [Deleted]
                       ... dark.
                       Emily Dickinson, from No. 55 Lines 1-4

26

Russell had chosen to wear the sports jacket with the large patches on the elbows. He had disliked the style when it first came out and disliked it more when it again had become fashionable a couple of years ago. "It makes you look professorish," Meredith had quipped when he had tried it on. It must have worked, because as he entered the meeting room at Drew University, a tall blonde woman immediately approached him from across the room.

"Professor Grayson?" she asked.

"I confess!" Russell answered, raising his arms in a gesture of surrender.

"So good to meet you at last! I'm Anna Marston."

"Ms Marston, how do you do?"

Her handshake was strong, nearly manly. Russell was certain that her strength had been acquired by twisting the arms of people like him to participate in her roundtable discussions.

"So glad you could come. I'm sure your perspective as a professor at Schuyler will prove enlightening to today's discussion."

"I hope so, but I may be overshadowed by the high-caliber professionals you've assembled on the panel."

"I doubt that will be the case. Terrible news from Newark, isn't it?" she asked, changing the subject.

"Terrible, but not surprising, I'm afraid," Russell responded. "Civil unrest has been increasing for a couple of years, now. Many people are frustrated. Those without effective, appropriate outlets, well, they often turn to violence, unfortunately. It's not just coincidence that Newark is again the stage for rioting."

"That's' a very objective assessment—almost cold," Anna said. Russell could sense she was taken aback by his comment.

"I'm not sure how you'd look at a riot in a warm light," he continued. "The violence is inexcusable, of course, but so are the policies that force many of these people into their plight. With every failure, the government offers more of the same policies as a remedy. The poorest—and the most desperate—are the first to feel their effects."

"So you're saying it's the government's fault?"

"Newark has been riot-free for fifty years, so, unlike some commentators, I don't think the residents there are born to be rioters. And I certainly don't wish to excuse individual decisions to become lawbreakers. But the politicians are constantly pitting one class against another and forcing all of us to identify with our economic class, like fans of some football team—without the option of changing teams. Repetition is an effective teaching tool. It's not surprising, then, that the people have learned what they've been repeatedly taught."

"I take it, then, that you are not a supporter of President Benson."

"You're very perceptive."

"But the Benson administration has done so much for education," Anna countered.

Russell studied Anna with interest. She was not the first he had encountered who overlooked the usurpation of freedom and the repetitive dismal failures in exchange for government largesse for a personal interest. The blindness of such people always made him appreciate Meredith's vision all the more. "Perhaps we should change the subject," he offered, "Politics can be a conversational minefield. I wonder, though, what payback we will get from investing in education when the entire civil society is disintegrating. What's happening in Newark is just the most visible cracks of that crumbling society."

"Okay, professor, but I think you overstate the case based upon the actions of a few miscreants." As she replied, a stocky man with a graying beard came up beside her. "Do you know Professor Daniels?" she asked.

"Call me Gil," the man said, shaking Russell's hand. "Professor Grayson. I've read your article in *Teaching American Literature*. Some very unorthodox approaches, I must say."

"There are several ways to skin a cat," Russell smiled. "And please, call me Russell."

"Perhaps. I must say, I'm envious of the freedom you enjoy at a small school like Schuyler."

"Are you suggesting that Rutgers has you laced up in some sort of straitjacket, Gil?"

"Each and every day the constraints become more narrow. Russell, we've just become units of labor fabricating a standardized, blister-packed product called a college education. There is no appreciation for variations in human minds, no tolerance for deviations in output."

"But at least there is output. The meat counter at my grocery store was nearly empty yesterday, and the prices of what is there are outrageous. Even hot dogs are becoming a pricey meal."

"I've noticed that, too," Gil responded. "Yet I had a steak at Montero's the other night that was excellent. Cost me a damn fortune, but tender as can be."

"Montero's? In Bergenfield?" Russell asked.

"That's right, just around the corner from

Schulyer."

"In my neighborhood, perhaps, but out of my league."

"I don't get there often, mind you. We splurged for my wife's birthday. Didn't think I'd have to take out a second mortgage—uh, make that a third!" Daniels laughed. It was the empty, heartless laugh Russell was hearing more often, as irony offered only a brief reprieve from stark reality.

They stood in an ornate room with pewter chandeliers and a pastoral mural painted on the walls above the chair rail. The oversized doorways were framed with massive woodwork, and the hardwood floors were covered with a huge rose colored rug with a geometric pattern. Russell took this all in as the speakers paused, not eager to continue the complaining that seemed to plague so many conversations lately. Nor was he eager to volunteer his school's limited history to comparisons with the nation's eighth oldest college.

Daniels nodded towards him slightly as Ms Marston led him away for another introduction. Russell moved to the panelist's dais to set down the materials he had brought with him. A few attendees had begun to drift into the room, although Russell had arrived nearly an hour early.

He took a seat behind his name card on the dais and arranged his few notes before him, then filled a water glass from the pitcher nearby. As inconspicuously as possible, he checked that the Glock was firmly secured in the ankle holster inside his right pants leg. A loud laugh from across the room caught his attention and also confirmed his conviction that he did not wish to engage in any more idle chatting. He took a sip of water and sat back to gaze, without any particular focus, out into the room.

When he spotted her, he was immediately interested. It wasn't her stature—she was no taller than the two women walking in with her. Nor was it her dress, although she was wearing a smart tan suit, while her companions were in athletic wear and sneakers. It was something about the way she carried herself. It reminded him of Meredith. This realization brought with it both a pang of loss, and intensified interest: was there anyone out there who could even begin to compare with his late wife?

She was animated; engaged in lively conversation with her companions. He saw her turn towards one of them and smile, a warm smile that again reminded him of his wife and his loss. He dropped his head to study his notes, but they were blurred by the tears that welled in his eyes. He blinked them away, and stared up at one of the chandeliers. In a few moments his eyesight cleared, and he returned to his notes and practiced in his imagination his remarks on making Shakespeare relevant in a world of increasing protest, anger, and violence.

"Professor Grayson? Monica Turner." The woman to his left extended her hand with the greeting. She had a sincere smile, and eyes that danced upon a face that had seen many seasons, a fact reinforced by the closely cropped gray hair that topped it.

"Nice to meet you," Russell said, taking her hand. "Dickinson High School, I believe?"

"Yes, for nearly forty years. I'm on the dais to represent the 'survivors.'" Her smile widened, and the positive impression Russell already had was further embellished.

"I thought the title 'survivor' was given to teachers who made it through the first semester in that neighborhood of Jersey City. Surely you have earned a higher ranking with that tenure!"

Monica chuckled and took her seat. "We have a bad 'rep,'" she said, "but the school is much better than what most people think. We have many *bona fide* students, and quite a few real scholars. The secret is to motivate and encourage them. I've had some success doing that."

Russell had read of Mrs. Turner's successes, even before he received the backgrounds of today's speakers that Anna had supplied. Her notoriety was affirmed almost annually in state education publications.

"Well I'm looking forward to learning some of your secrets, as I'm sure most in the audience will as well."

"You're very kind," she said. Russell thought he detected a slight blush in her face. "My secret is to stay fresh, which is why I am here: to learn, to assimilate, to apply."

Russell felt fortunate to have such a professional next to him. That would surely make the day more enjoyable. Even as he thought this, his eyes were pulled away as they caught a glimpse of the brown-haired woman across the room, leaning gracefully down from her chair to retrieve a notebook from her briefcase. It took a concentrated effort to return his look to his companion.

* * * *

The seminar progressed much as Russell had imagined it would. Monica was the first to speak, hers being an inspirational address, suggesting a diversity of approaches was the key to success. Only by having a varied arsenal at her disposal was she capable of finding the right combination of unique approaches to match to the special challenges that some students offered. Russell was amused when she suggested that many students were taken aback when the short, gray-haired stereotypical English teacher would on occasion employ street jive to translate a passage of Chaucer.

When his time came, Russell offered specific examples of methods he had used for improving students' reading comprehension, helping them to make inferences, and articulating their thoughts in written essays. He was gratified when his remarks received enthusiastic applause, and he was especially appreciative when Monica gave him a nod of approval as she clapped her hands.

To his surprise, he fielded more than his share of inquiries during the question and answer period. When the woman in the tan suit he had noticed earlier stood to pose her question, he couldn't understand why he felt a lump form in his throat. The sensation only seemed to intensify when he heard her question and recognized that it was more insightful than most he had answered.

"Professor Grayson: while I recognize the innovations some of your methodologies employ, do you not sense that some of the accomplishments you achieve come at the expense of legitimate standards of academic excellence?"

Russell considered his response for a moment before answering. "I would suggest," he said, "that critics of the methodologies make a distinction between tactics designed to encourage student engagement with strategies to develop competent reading, writing, and analysis skills. I can assure you that the standards of all English composition courses at Schuyler, regardless of the themes or related studies that are associated with them, have not been compromised and will continue to remain unchanged. Clear, concise, and insightful use of the language—which implies consistent adherence to the rules of grammar and the artistic elements of composition—are, first and foremost, standards by which the students' work is judged.

"On the other hand, many of the topics I covered today involve devices to encourage students to accept the assigned texts as relevant to their lives and competent as a means of improving their skills and knowledge base. Once a student has 'signed on' to the program, more traditional educational methodologies hold sway. Without that initial acceptance, however, little headway can be made in the traditional educational sense. A student has no incentive to explore the 'how' of an essay's composition if he is too busy questioning the 'why' of the assignment in the first place. We can bemoan the decline of pure scholarship during the past few decades, but that does not change the fact that the students coming into our classrooms lack such a purist's drive. Blaming the secondary schools such as yours, which is—?"

"Wallington High School," the woman answered.

"—such as Wallington High School, is not totally fair, either. Certainly the primary schools share some of the blame, as do the parents, and, of course, the media which constantly bombards our youth. I think it's only fitting that in several examples I presented earlier, I have turned the media against its normal bent, using it as a tool to encourage scholarship rather than to sabotage it."

Russell felt more than the usual level of satisfaction when the questioner sat down, and smiled in acknowledgement of his response.

* * * *

After the seminar concluded, Russell was walking across the parking lot towards his car when he again spotted the Wallington High School teacher. She was standing beside a silver Honda Civic, appearing frustrated as she flung her cell phone into her purse.

"Problem?" he asked.

"Oh, I can't reach my husband, and my car won't start. I need to pick up my daughter at school, and I'm late already."

"Your daughter's at Wallington?"

"No, Garfield High. That's where we live."

"That's on my way. I'm heading back to Schuyler; I can give you a lift if you'd like."

The woman considered his offer for just a moment. "You sure it's no bother?"

"Not at all."

"I'd really appreciate it, Professor Grayson."

"Russell. My car's right over there."

"I'm Linda. Linda Norton."

Soul, Wilt thou toss again?
Emily Dickinson, from No. 139

27

Michael turned onto his street and let out a sigh of relief. It had been a difficult day, beginning with his run in with Alberto's goons. A trip to the north end of his territory and more than usual traffic congestion had not helped. Finally, Rudy reported that a shipment had been delayed, and he was unable to fill half of Michael's orders.

Michael pulled the truck around to the rear of the house, being even more circumspect than usual. He had no neighbors especially close to his house. Still, he always tried to make the maneuver with no eyes present, keeping his less than legal enterprise a little more private. Now with his involvement with Alberto, he felt an increased need for secrecy.

After plugging his truck's refrigeration unit into his house current, Michael walked back around to the front of his house, retrieving his cell phone from his shirt pocket as he walked. Dead again. The phone's battery was not holding a charge, and in two trips to the cellular phone store he had been unable to obtain a replacement. "Out of stock" was becoming too common a refrain of many merchants, and it appeared he would join them tomorrow.

Passing in front of his garage, Michael looked up when a green Forester pulled into the driveway. He didn't recognize the vehicle, and his heart began to beat faster. Then he saw Linda seated in the passenger seat, and as soon as the vehicle stopped, Liz stepped out of a rear door.

"Hey, Dad!" she cried. "We're late for my doctor's appointment," she added as she flung open the overhead door and dropped her book bag next to the door to the kitchen. Linda was stepping out of the car as was the driver, a neatly dressed professional-type with thinning brown hair.

"Hi, Hon," Linda said. "I tried to call you but got no answer."

"Yeah, my cell's dead again." Michael's focus was on the driver and he barely glanced in his wife's direction.

"My car wouldn't start at Drew. Fortunately, Russell came to the rescue. Russell Grayson, this is my husband, Michael."

The stranger had taken some steps towards Michael, but stopped abruptly when Michael thrust his hands in his hip pockets and gave him an icy glare. The stranger seemed to fumble for words for an instant before saying, "It was no trouble, really. It was right on my way back to the college."

"College?" Michael asked.

"Yes, Schuyler University. I teach English there."

"Mom!" Liz interjected, "If we miss my spot in line we'll be there all night, and I've got a ton of homework."

"I've got to run. Thank you again, Professor Grayson."

"My pleasure, Linda. Let me move my car out of your way."

The professor paused to look at Michael one last time, but Michael offered him no comfort. Michael felt the wave of heat swell upward and believed his face must be glowing red. He gave the stranger a slight nod—more of an approving acknowledgement that he was leaving than a thank you for delivering his wife and daughter home. Michael stepped off the driveway to allow his wife to back out of the garage. When the professor gave her a farewell wave before driving off, Michael felt the anger shift to rage.

The memory was vivid although years had passed. He still owned his own deli then, and had closed up early to surprise Linda at her "Back to School Night." A quick inquiry at the first classroom he passed inside the school's main doors had given him the directions he needed, and Michael had walked through the halls stealthily, hoping to see her surprise when she looked up to see him sitting among a classroom of unfamiliar parents.

As so often happened, reality had fallen far short of his fantasies. The hallways were crowded with parents passing between classes. Michael was more than a classroom away when he spotted Linda, standing in the hallway next to her classroom door.

She was beautiful, of course. He always thought she was beautiful. When he had first seen her at a high school dance, he had been dumbstruck. For more than an hour he had stared at her, finally building up the courage to ask her to dance. He had been sure she would decline. Mortals such as he had no business communing with the gods, especially when his mortality was further insulted by being the only son of a maintenance man at an apartment complex.

But she had said yes. Not just to the dance, but for many dates afterward. She even had said yes to his proposal of marriage despite her father's objections to his humble background and uncertain future lacking any particular skill or career prospect. Her father was an established attorney in Morristown, and had looked down his nose at Michael from the beginning. As the couple's relationship grew stronger, the barrister's disdain became more obvious. Only Linda's mother, an incurable romantic from whom Linda obtained her good looks, argued in Michael's behalf and was successful in vacating her husband's order that Linda should see Michael no longer.

Seeing her standing by her classroom door, Michael had been taken once again by her joyful attitude characterized by her wide smile. His adulation cooled, however, when he sensed that her joy was the result of camaraderie with a fellow teacher, a young man with an air of sophistication he carried well above his inherent good looks. Michael had stepped behind a bank of lockers, from where he maintained a vigil that quickly confirmed what he had immediately suspected: that his wife truly enjoyed this teacher's company, and as a result of it, she appeared to glow even more than was her usual nature.

When the bell had rung and Linda had retreated to her classroom—but not before exchanging yet one more pleasantry with her scholastic neighbor—Michael had abandoned his plan, and instead had returned home. On his drive there, his anger had grown to fury and then to rage. Perhaps if Liz had been home, her presence might have tempered Michael somewhat. But she was at a friend's house, and the empty Norton abode only served to accentuate his feeling of loneliness and despair. His wrath erupted and no personal belonging or sentimental memento was safe from his tantrum. The destruction had not been complete, but it was focused, and its effect had been devastating to his spouse when she returned home later. Michael shuddered to think what effect it might also have had on his then twelve-year-old daughter.

Perhaps because of this reflection, Michael did not enter the house, but chose instead to walk up the street. His strides were long, as if he were eager to reach his destination. He had no goal, however, but selected streets randomly, walking almost two miles before turning to return, using the distance and the cool late afternoon autumn air in combination to cool his frenzy. He was almost calm by the time he returned home, bending to pick-up the newspaper on his front porch. Bold headlines had been common lately, and today's were not any different in style although the message was in a slightly different vein: Death Toll Exceeds 400 in Tampa Terrorist Attack.

The ... **[Deleted]**
 ... hold –
 Emily Dickinson, from No. 281 Lines 9-10

28

"So, how did it go?"

Russell was not surprised, but was nevertheless amused when Lenny stuck his head into his office soon after Russell arrived back on campus.

"Very well, I think," Russell replied. "My presentation was warmly received, and I got more than my share of the Q and A time."

"Gil Daniels was there from Rutgers?"

"Yes, he was."

"Not surprising. He seems to get to a lot of the programs like that. How was his presentation?"

"A bit on the conservative side; nothing earth shattering or especially innovative."

"Good. Very good. Keeping Schuyler on the cutting edge—excellent!"

And just as quickly, he was gone. Russell shook his head and laughed softly to himself as he considered his eccentric dean. He turned back to his desk and fired up his computer as he dialed his phone for his voice mail messages. The second message, from Jeff Downs, grabbed his attention. He immediately dialed him back.

"Hello," came the coarse voice on the other end.

"Mr. Downs, it's Russell Grayson. I see you called?"

"Oh, hey there, professor. Yeah, I've got some information for you. Hold on; let me take this in my office." Russell heard some rustling and scratching sounds and Jeff's voice in the background. "Dolores, love, would you hang this up after I pick up in the office?"

In a less than a minute, Jeff was on the phone again. "Okay...right. Well, not surprisingly our Alberto is well known to my law enforcement sources. Alberto Dominic Gonzalez. Born and raised in Paterson, he's a bit of a mutt. P.R. father; mother was a free-spirited daughter of a lieutenant in the Columbo Crime Family. You can imagine what kind of waves her marriage to a Hispanic created in that culture. Still, Alberto's dad was a straight arrow; came to own a legit laundry business. Ditto for his mom, no problems with the law.

"Alberto was a different matter, though. In and out of the juvie system several times before he was eighteen. In his first year as an adult he was charged with stealing a car, one count of extortion, and an A&B rap."

"'A&B?'" Russell questioned.

"Sorry. Assault and Battery. Yeah, so the car heist was thrown out on a technicality, the victim dropped charges on the extortion, and Alberto received probation on the assault. It's been a few years, of course, but I bumped into the cop who pinched him for the assault. He was a rookie when he made the collar, but he remembers very well the details of the case. Seems Alberto had a high-priced suit representing him. The copper says he remembers the prosecutor telling him Alberto's lawyer usually handled mob cases. Maybe Alberto's grandpa had a warm spot for the kid. Who knows? Anyway, it was a knifing incident, and both the cop and prosecutor were amazed that he got off with just probation.

"So our boy continued, progressing up the penal code ladder, but never serving any serious time. Meanwhile, he was building something of his own little syndicate, but unlike his mother's side of the family, this one was multi-ethnic. A real equal employment opportunity mafia.

"Fast forward to about a year ago. The county Major Crime Task Force collars our boy for a laundry list of violations. By all accounts it was a good bust: solid evidence, no Fifth Amendment hanky-panky.

"You've heard the well-worn saw: 'a prosecutor can get a grand jury to indict a ham sandwich', he's got so much control over the proceedings? Well the young prosecutor assigned Alberto's case couldn't get an indictment! Not one true bill on any count! Alberto walks on the whole package! And the prosecutor? Suddenly, he's gone—last seen practicing real estate law in Vineland!"

Russell absorbed this stream of information with amazement. His perception of the criminal justice system had always been one of a structured, invariable, and respectable protector of civil society. Now, in one case, the case that seems to have impacted him personally so strongly, it appeared that the system was very fallible, and possibly manipulated by unknown powers.

"What do you think that means? Did Alberto's attorney some how manage to get him off again?" Russell asked.

"Not likely. The defendant's not represented before the Grand Jury. Grand Jury tampering is not only difficult because of the large number of jurors, but also extremely risky if you get caught. No, my hunch is someone in the government didn't want Alberto indicted. Someone higher than the MCU, which reports to the prosecutor. I'm guessing Alberto's got friends in the state attorney general's office…or the feds."

"So what do we do now?" Russell queried.

"What do you want to do? You want to put a tail on him? That'll be expensive and I'm not sure it'll be very productive. Let me remind you that I'm retired, and not eager to come out of retirement to risk pissing off this kind of muscle. Still, if that's what you want to do, I've e-mailed you his LKA, er, last known address, a photo, and some other stuff. Not sure how eager another p.i. will be to take this on. Just be careful, my man. This guy doesn't play nice and his soldiers may be worse."

"Okay, well thanks again Mr. Downs, for your help, and your advice."

"Hey, no problem. Kept me out of my wife's garden for a day. The woman loves to dig! Uh, oh. She's giving me the evil eye as I speak. Probably has some bulbs she wants dug up before the first frost. You be safe, professor."

As Russell hung up the phone, he considered what he should do with the information Downs had provided. Wisdom suggested he give Alberto a wide berth. But Meredith deserved more.

On his way to Down's e-mail message, headline news filled Russell's computer screen. The lead story was how belated deaths from the Tampa terror attack had exceeded four hundred. Russell's eyes were grabbed by a headline among the secondary stories: Syria Surges into West Bank; Anti-aircraft Fire Brings down U.S. Jet.

At ... **[Deleted]**
... Defeat,
Emily Dickinson, from No. 172 Lines 10-11

29

"Take this into your father," Linda said, handing Liz the McDonald's bag. She hated to spend money on fast food, but it was getting late and she knew Michael would be hungry. As Liz had predicted, missing their appointment time at the doctor's office had cost them dearly. Collecting her briefcase and other belongings from the back seat, Linda entered the kitchen to find Michael removing a Big Mac from the paper bag.

"Sorry, Mike. It was so late when we got out of the doctor's office. Liz and I already ate."

"It's all right," he said, hardly looking up at her.

"Everything okay?" she asked.

"Yeah, fine," he answered, retrieving some stray French fries from the bottom of the bag.

Linda sensed some tension, but thinking it might just be hunger, she stepped into the adjoining family room to unload her arms.

" 'Was nice of the professor to bring you home," Michael said around a mouthful of Big Mac.

"Yes, it was." She detected a slight bite in her husband's words. As she had learned to do over the years, she chose not to react and to allow him to work out his issue in his own good time. "Oh," she added, "I better call Tony to see if he can tow my car in tomorrow."

"I'm surprised he was willing to drive this far out of the way."

"It wasn't that far."

"First to the high school, then here?"

"Mike, what are you trying to say?" Linda asked impatiently.

"I'm just saying…seems like he was going out of his way to help you out."

"There are some nice people left in the world, Mike."

"Especially those that are looking for something—"

"Mike, it was *nothing*. I was at the conference; he was at the conference. My car died; his car didn't. He offered me a lift. That was it."

"Mm-hmm," Michael said, stuffing a couple of French fries into his mouth.

"I am so *sick* of this! You question me about everyone I meet, like I'm some kind of trollop. Why are you so jealous? I'm not cheating on you. I wouldn't do that. I'm *happy* here!"

Linda took a step towards her husband, but he grabbed the paper bag containing the French fries off the counter, and stepped away.

"Yeah, happy."

"It's true!"

Michael lowered his voice, and looked into the hallway, apparently conscious that Liz was somewhere in the house. He seemed indifferent as to whether she overheard this argument. With a shift in topic, however, he put up his guard.

"Happy with me, the common criminal?" he hissed.

"Mike—"

"Happy with me, Michael Norton, Garfield High School Class of '95? Who can't put two freakin' sentences together that wouldn't be all marked up with that red pen of yours! Who'd embarrass you if I went with you to one of these— these seminars where college professors hang out!"

"Mike, I'm not embarrassed by you," Linda

119

pleaded. "I love you. For who you are, for who you've always been."

"How could you not be embarrassed?" he asked, his voice rising in volume. Quickly, he brought it back in check. "I sneak around during the day and lie low at night. Selling black market meat—and associating with creepy hoodlums."

"Mike, stop talking like that. It's just for a short time. This economy has to improve someday."

"I could lose this job tomorrow, the whole thing could be shut down by a health inspector here—or a state trooper in Wisconsin—or a zillion cops in between. Or Alberto can squeeze even more outta me. Or I could be fuckin' arrested. Then where'd you be?"

"But I'm here for you, now and always." Linda was trying desperately to defuse the situation.

"Bull! Don't tell me you're not tempted by some college professor with his preppy little jacket and fancy words!" Michael's voice dropped to a whisper. "One little failure in bed, and, and you hop into this asshole's car!"

"Michael—"

"It's bull, Linda!" Michael stomped on the pedal of the trash can near the garage door, causing the lid to fly open. He slammed the bag into the trash, then did the same to the door as he left the kitchen for the garage.

Linda stood motionless, her eyes closed. *Here we go again.*

Goodbye ... ***[Deleted]***
... know –
Emily Dickinson, from No. 279 Lines 13-14

30

Rufus rushed past his master, the dog's weight forcing the man's legs aside as he did so. Russell was in no mood to play, and let the retriever run into the yard on his own. Upon the dog's return, Russell closed the door behind his pet, whose hindquarters were nearly thrown out of alignment by the exuberance of its wagging tail. As preoccupied as he was, Russell could not avoid smiling at his companion, and vigorously scratched behind the dog's ears.

Russell moved through the house to the study and brought his computer to life. Impatiently, too agitated to sit, he stood behind his chair as he waited for the machine to boot and for his e-mail program to run. He was relieved immediately, almost incapacitated, when he saw the message header with his daughter's screen name, Eaglerider, attached. She was alive. He sat down and opened the message.

Hi Dad,
You may have heard how market forces have depressed one of our product lines. I am confident that we will bounce back from this setback. The salesman involved has been assigned to another product, happy that his short rough ride is over.
I personally sold several tons of product to some difficult customers, and they are much better for it. Will be glad when this sales campaign is over and I can come

home and see you again.
> Love,
> Karen

Russell's relief was quickly tempered with the understanding that Karen would be at risk again tomorrow. He closed his eyes and offered a fervent prayer for her safety.

Much as his thoughts were with his fighter-pilot daughter, Russell could not keep from thinking about his earlier phone conversation with Jeff Downs. He opened the e-mail from the detective and promptly clicked the icons for the attachments.

The mug shot that stared back at him from the computer screen was that of a defiant man, a cynical smirk contorting his lips. In an unbiased setting, the man might have appeared handsome and well groomed. But in the harsh light of insinuation—as one-sided, anonymous, and perhaps circumstantial as it might be—he appeared to Russell as a monster. As such, the image was seared into Russell's brain such that he was certain he would never need to refer to the hardcopy print he plucked off his printer.

Russell read the narratives from the incident and arrest reports, imagining him at the crime scenes, trying to piece together the pieces of the puzzle as the police officers had done. Repeatedly, Russell recognized the common elements. Alberto worked alone, or with very little help, and he never kept his identity a secret. He seemed so different from the hooded gunman and his similarly disguised accomplices who had gunned down John Landers, Meredith, and the others in that Fort Wayne auditorium. Could he be the same man? Had he become more prudent, more careful as his criminal life matured? Were the stakes—a capital crime, the cold-blooded murder of a well-known personality—so high as to demand a different methodology?

And what would be Alberto's motivation? "Motive" they always called it on the crime shows.

What would cause him, this product of the Garden State, to hop a plane to Indiana and commit such a heinous act? How did Landers—much less Meredith, sweet, innocent Meredith—threaten Alberto or his little neighborhood empire?

"I'm guessing Alberto's got friends in the state attorney general's office...or the feds." Downs's words echoed in Russell's head. Why would an upper-level law enforcement official act to help this thuggish criminal? Unless...Unless it was to create an indebtedness. An obligation to perform a task so unsavory, so alien to the normal course of things: an assassination.

Russell felt a sudden chill and rose from his chair. Walking to the window, he looked out into the back yards of his neighbors, and took in the suburban landscape, which could be the stereotype background for a mural depicting life in America. Seen in the dimming dusk, the banality of the congruent plots, the sameness of the trees planted by the subdivision's contractor, the scruffy remains of summer garden plots, the duplication of children's swing sets here, there, and over there, too—these stark commonalities were shaded but not obscured. The democracy of the scene was overpowering and, in a way, depressing. In striving to attain some independent, personal space, he and his neighbors had replicated to a great degree so many shared "must haves" and typical common denominators.

Russell sighed, and deplored the oppressive nature of such conformity. He smiled as he recalled how he had seldom worked on writing his books here in his study. He remembered Meredith asking why he had to drive to the campus to work when he had everything he needed here. "I just feel more inspired at Schuyler," he had said. But even then he had been skeptical. He could not legitimately compare his limited view of the college's grounds to Shelley's Sussex, Wordsworth's Cumberland, or the Bard's walled gardens in Stratford, or even to the crowded streets and alleys of London.

But Meredith's voice filled his head. *"To be free includes the possibility of being free to be mediocre. Fortunately, freedom has often facilitated brilliance."* She was never an apologist for the free market, but rather an advocate for its superiority to all of the alternatives. Its failures, she would suggest, were more often failures of man's short-sightedness or distorted values rather than a systemic shortcoming. What was needed was not restrictions on economic freedoms, but an expansion of religious and ethical awareness, something much more likely in a free society where tolerance of opposing views is encouraged.

Ronna Gordon's face appeared in Russell's mind. He had not thought of her for some time. He remembered the meetings that the college opened to the public, where her open opposition to "Green Science" had been aired. Meredith had appeared in her behalf, speaking of academic freedom and the nature of dissenting views in such an environment. His wife had taken some heat for that position, and Russell remembered how he had been relieved that he had not become involved. Dr. Gordon ultimately was dismissed, the show trial being the justification to which the university's board of governors merely applied their seal. Russell remembered vividly Ronna's farewell remarks to Meredith, which he had been present to hear. *"It's bad science, Meredith. I will not—I cannot—sacrifice my intellectual integrity and endorse it. It was good science—the freedom to question, the obligation to hypothesize, the inherent integrity of the experiments' results—that liberated us from the selfish monarchs and the intolerant clergy. It will be bad science—where discipline is forsaken and theories go unchallenged—that will return us to dark ages, tyranny, and oppression."*

Rufus nuzzled Russell's hand, and the man

returned from his daydream. The dog's loyalty and honest devotion was a trait missing in too many men nowadays. To what ends would dishonest men go? Were there any boundaries?

Russell sat and absentmindedly pet the dog. He recalled reading an article recently reporting that several electric generating companies were urging repeal of the "green taxes" that had been levied a half dozen years ago. The author had been sympathetic to maintaining them, even as he had to admit that the dire predictions made back then had not come to pass. Just as Ronna Gordon had said would happen. *"In the early seventies, we were headed towards a new Ice Age; today it's Global Warming,"* she had said. Russell recalled as well that it was West Virginia that closely followed California into formal bankruptcy, the result of the collapse of coal prices. Apparently well-intentioned limitations imposed on export coal had resulted in the total collapse of the state's coal industry, already under immense competitive pressure from low-sulfur coal from Nebraska's Powder River Basin. With the loss of an export market, most mines closed, unemployment skyrocketed, and tax revenues plummeted. Meredith had predicted this calamity, and Russell remembered how a lecture she had presented on the topic had ended in chaos after being disrupted by an organized group of environmentalists. She had actually been hurt slightly as the protest became ugly, bruised in a tug-of-war for the lectern. The incident was reported in the national media, and had led to John Landers learning of the passionate Schuyler economics professor.

Russell looked again at the printouts in his hand and a thought came to him. He had no classes tomorrow. He turned to his computer and typed "Lance Bloom Vineland attorney" into his search engine.

The ...
   [Deleted]
         ... die!
      Emily Dickinson, from No. 235 Lines 1-4

31

She was young and attractive. Her dark skin seemed to glow with just-scrubbed freshness, and her black hair was trimmed into a tight frame around her round face. Russell thought she was little older than his typical student, and was quietly impressed that she was the sole assistant to Lance Bloom, Esquire.

Russell had had a considerable amount of time to reach such a judgment. Arriving at the modest office accessed from a quiet brick courtyard just off Landis Avenue in central Vineland, Russell had seen her work for more than three hours. He heard her fingers dancing across the keyboard as he finished reading the magazine he brought. He saw her escort clients into her boss's office as he skimmed the few sailing magazines arrayed on the waiting room coffee table. He overheard telephone conversations where she sounded familiar with the clients' cases, providing answers in several instances without troubling Bloom. Now, she was once again attempting to be graciously hospitable despite the clear intent of the attorney to be otherwise.

"Are you sure I can't get you some coffee or water or something?"

"No, thanks. I'm fine," Russell answered.

Emma—Russell had heard her name several times earlier—moved to the kitchenette and shut down the coffee maker and cleaned up for the end of the day. When she had finished, she stepped into the attorney's office and closed the door. Even though the voices were muffled, he could discern that the fact that he still remained in the waiting area was the subject of the conversation.

When she stepped out of the office, Emma put on a trim leather jacket and smiled pleasantly at Russell as she said good night. Russell glanced at his watch and noted it was precisely five o'clock.

Fifteen minutes later, Bloom exited his office, wearing a tan trench coat and carrying a leather briefcase.

"I'm sorry I wasn't able to see you today, but as I told you on the phone, and as my secretary advised you when you got here, there were no openings in my schedule." Motioning toward the door, Bloom made no eye contact with Russell as he added, "Now, if you'll excuse me, I'm afraid I must close the office."

"Mr. Bloom, this will just take a minute or less," Russell offered, rising from his chair.

"I'm sorry, but I have an appointment." The attorney still did not look at Russell as he opened the door to usher him out.

Russell stood his ground. "It's about Alberto Gonzalez," he said.

"Yes, yes. You said as much earlier. But I really must be going. If you please…"

"I have reason to believe he murdered my wife…" Russell said.

For the first time Lance Bloom looked at Russell, at the same time dropping his arms, the heavy briefcase dragging them down in further resignation. Russell thought he saw a flash of panic in the barrister's eyes.

"I'm…I'm sorry for your loss. But I don't know how I can help you. Please, I *must* insist that you leave now so I can lock up."

"…and four others," Russell continued, "including John Landers."

Bloom turned away with a nervous twitch, and stared into the courtyard. Momentarily he closed the door and motioned Russell to follow him back into his office. Once Russell stepped inside, Bloom closed the door behind him.

"Grand Jury proceedings are completely confidential. I am sworn to secrecy. There is nothing I can tell you about his case without violating legal or ethical codes."

"I'm not asking anything about the proceedings," Russell asserted. "I'm asking about something outside the courtroom, outside the norm, and most likely outside the law." Russell glared at Bloom. He sensed that he had him trapped, cornered between lies that had laced him up more neatly than a spider enshrouding a helpless moth at the corner of its web.

"You don't know what you're asking. You don't know who you're dealing with."

"That's what I'm trying to find out," Russell said. "Give me a name and I'll be on my way."

Bloom scoffed at the comment and tossed his briefcase into one of the guest chairs. "Like I said, you have no idea who you're dealing with."

Russell's glare remained unchanged.

"These people have unlimited resources, boundless reach," Bloom continued. "They've made it clear—my life, or my wife's or kid's—all are in danger if I whisper a word to anyone."

"And what about my wife?" Russell asked. "Didn't you once take a hallowed oath to protect her life, too?"

Bloom turned his back on Russell and walked to the window that looked out onto the street. The lights of the town were on now and provided a fantasy backdrop to the ruthless reality of the small law office with the uniform volumes of West law books lining the shelves on one wall.

"You're a fool," Bloom said at last. "Believe

me when I tell you these people are too strong to tangle with. What do you expect to accomplish by going against them?"

Russell was taken aback by this comment. He had never questioned what he was looking to accomplish, or why the mysterious phone calls had set him into motion without a clear vision of a goal.

"Justice?" Russell volunteered, the word falling like a solitary dime onto the office carpet, so empty did it sound.

"Yeah, right!" Bloom threw back sarcastically. "Lady Justice is blindfolded, and a lot goes on behind her back—and in front of her, too, for that matter—which she never knows about."

The room became very quiet, and Russell became aware of a clock on the desk, ticking away the seconds precisely, unendingly.

"Look," Russell continued, "I don't know what I'm doing, exactly. But I do know that I owe it to my wife to…, to at least understand why she died. To find out who thinks they benefited from her loss…from my loss.

"You say you're married," he continued. "Can't you understand that? Can't you imagine yourself in my place?"

The attorney turned around from the window and faced Russell. For the first time Bloom's eyes were looking directly at Russell. Russell thought they looked moist.

"I imagine being in your place every day," Bloom said at last. "Which is why I can't—I won't—name names. Now please, leave. Leave now."

Russell felt the complete helplessness of the situation. He felt the interminable drabness of the ride down the Garden State Parkway, and regretted the need to return north tonight. He felt the chill of knowing Meredith's death would remain not vindicated, not avenged. Reaction to this chill sparked a new fire.

"Answer me this, and this only, then: State or Feds?"

Bloom shook his head silently.

"Come on. You speak of your oaths and your ethics. Do something right for my wife! Tell me one simple truth!"

"Feds," Bloom mouthed, though the word itself was unspoken.

You ...
   [Deleted]
      ... wake –
         Emily Dickinson, from No. 156 Lines 1-3

32

Linda awoke as Michael slipped quietly under the covers. The clock read 2:37. It had been more than six hours since he had stormed out of the kitchen. She lay silently, her back towards him. Turning her back on Michael was something she had never intended to do and still did not wish to do. Yet this latest outburst was troubling, and she remembered clearly what it was like, years before, to come home to the house trashed.

She remembered picking up the picture frame. Its shattered glass both masked the image of the smiling couple behind it and revealed the truth that their relationship was badly fractured. She had picked up the body of the small china fawn and its head in the far corner of the room. It was a small trinket, something he had purchased when they had vacationed in the Adirondacks. But she remembered he had secretly bought it after seeing that she had admired it as she roamed through the little shop on her own. Later, when she found it gift-wrapped on her pillow, she was moved at how it represented his awareness and his thoughtfulness. Holding the pieces in her hand, she had felt a loss as if the inexpensive curio were a priceless work of art and as if her husband were the most reprehensible among men.

She had risked so much for Michael. The concerns of her friends, the objections of her father, her own disbelief in the merging of their two different worlds, all these memories returned and forced her to question how well grounded her relationship with Michael was. Had she allowed the appeal of romanticism to overpower the cautions of her more conservative leanings? Had the dashing Lord Byron completely pushed aside the stodgy John Milton?

Perhaps so. But she had done so willingly. She had believed it all so honestly. And now her Don Juan had destroyed her house, slammed the door, and walked away from her and the life they had built together.

Even as she felt her heart was broken in two, Linda's mothering instinct had kicked in. By a most unusual quirk of fate, she had arrived home before Liz returned from her friend's house. Linda rushed to clean up the mess and return the house to as close to normal as she could. When Liz bounded in the door, Linda had led her to the couch. Holding her close, she told her that her parents had "had an argument."

Ever independent, Liz had squirmed out of Linda's embrace and faced her mother, defiance animating her eyes. "Where is he? I want to talk to him," she had said.

"He's left. I don't know where he is. I have to think he wants to be alone."

"I want to see him! Where is he? This isn't fair!"

"You're right. It isn't fair—"

"Daddy loves me. He wouldn't leave me!"

"I know your father loves you—I'm sure of it. But today he's hurt you, and he's hurt me. We can be sad; we should be sad. But we can't allow ourselves to be hurt, either. Someday—I hope someday soon—we can talk about what happened today calmly, rationally, as a family."

It hadn't been soon. Michael and Linda's next meeting was contentious and spiteful. Michael became angry when Linda told him that she would not allow Liz to see him in his current state of mind.

Next came attorney consultations, and later, a refereed meeting on visitation. There Michael was much more restrained, having been advised by his attorney, no doubt, that the slightest eruption of bad temper might bar him from seeing Liz again.

Linda wasn't sure what might have caused such a change in Michael. Many months of unemployment had not helped. She recalled how frustrated he had become with few offers of work and what seemed the inevitable rejections that came after he applied. Businesses reacted to declines in sales and rising costs by rejecting unionized workers whenever they could. This was especially true in transportation, where non-union truckers grabbed business away from the unionized carriers. Michael's membership in the Teamsters proved nearly useless, as the union concentrated on maintaining the agreements they had rather than the futile exercise of attempting to grow.

Once, out of desperation, Michael had gone to Paterson early one morning, joining a group of anxious day laborers to see what contractors might show up with a need for strong backs. With a little pleading he had obtained work. His co-workers were mostly Mexicans, and Michael sensed that they were talking about him and making fun of him in their private dialect. "Accidents" occurred throughout the morning, and one of the men used these occasions to taunt Michael. These challenges increased until after lunch when Michael could tolerate them no longer. The wrestling match that followed resulted in Michael being fired on the spot with his pay being forfeited, forcing him to return home by bus from the worksite.

Michael had been philosophical afterwards. He said he realized that his employment was probably excluding a relative of one or more of the others, and that they were acting as a unit to protect each other. He understood what was going on, although he had never before experienced anything like it.

Linda also had seen the effects of similar stress on her friends' relationships. Foreclosures, divorces, unemployment austerity, relocating to other states—all these she had seen, often more than once. Shoppers in the stores seemed more rude, drivers on the roads more ruthless. The newspapers reported instances of road rage along with what seemed to be an ever increasing number of senseless killings.

Divorce settlement papers were ready for signing when Michael called Linda and confessed that separation was not what he truly desired. Eventually, Linda admitted the same thing. He took her out to dinner, and once again proved to be the thoughtful, caring man she had loved at first and for most of their marriage. The evening ended in their bedroom.

They marked their formal reunion with a recitation of their marriage vows. Linda had recovered the VHS tape of their wedding from a drawer in the buffet, next to her mother's silver service. From it she had typed out their parts, and they read them to each other, solemnly and with added meaning as Liz looked on, tears of joy in her eyes. A champagne toast followed, with Liz joining in, although her request for a refill was denied.

Now Linda lay with her back to Michael. She imagined him lying on his back, his arms crossed over his chest, his eyes to the ceiling. He could be defiant. He could be obstinate. And he could also be tender. He could also be caring. To bridge the abyss between these extremes, Linda imagined not a tight rope, across which she must carefully tread, but rather a solid, masonry sculpture, that vaulted the valley atop dozens of symmetrical arches. It was a viaduct, beautiful and elegant, yet strong enough to withstand river torrents, cyclonic winds, and the gradual insults of variable weather. She imagined herself the architect of that bridge, charged with the task of fitting each stone securely in place. And she must begin building now.

    Linda rolled over and placed her head on his shoulder and held him firmly with her arm.

We ... ***[Deleted]***
... away –
Emily Dickinson, from No. 419 Lines 1-2

33

Liz always felt a little skip in her heartbeat when she approached Chris's locker each morning. She would usually find him there, horsing around with Jason whose locker was a few feet away. Jason, an offensive lineman for the Bulldog's football team, was one of Chris's best friends, and during football season, the relationship seemed to be cemented even more tightly. The two were still coasting on a high—the result of last Saturday's upset victory, thanks in part to Chris catching a touchdown pass. The final game of the season would be tomorrow, Thanksgiving Day, and Liz was sure the two would have difficulty containing their nervous energy.

Liz was excited, too, for other reasons. Four days off from school was in store, and she was looking forward to that. Most importantly, Chris and she had planned a little clandestine rendezvous after tomorrow's game.

She was disappointed to round the corner only to see Jason, alone, leaning against his locker studying a paper.

"Hi, Jason."

"Hey, Liz," he answered, looking up.

"You seen Chris?"

"Yeah, he's around. Left a few minutes ago."

"Oh?" Chris made a habit of beginning his day here, and Liz hoped it was because he looked forward to seeing her.

"Something's not right with Chris," Jason

offered, lowering his voice and looking around for eavesdroppers.

"What do you mean?"

"I don't know. It just wasn't like usual. Something's bugging him. Talk to him, Liz."

Liz made the rounds of likely places to find Chris. The gym, his first period math class, even the Guidance Office. She couldn't find him anywhere. Her inquiries were met with shrugs and shakes of the head. Finally, the bell rang, and she had to give up and begin her school day.

* * * *

She spotted him in the hall on his way to third period U.S. History, the one class they shared. "Where have you been? I've been looking all over for you."

"Hey," he said, giving her a hug and pulling her out of the center of the hallway.

"What's the matter? Jason said something's up."

Chris leaned back against the lockers and exhaled heavily. He turned to Liz and smiled weakly, but she thought she saw his lips tremble.

"It's my uncle Phil," he said. "The bank wants to take his house."

"That sucks," Liz responded.

"Yeah. Since he lost his job, he's been having trouble making payments."

"So what's going to happen?"

"Well, that's the thing. He asked my dad to help him out. And, of course, he will. But Dad's using the money he saved for my college....I won't be going to Gettysburg next year."

It felt like the floor collapsed under Liz's feet. Chris had been looking forward to next year. He had even met with the football coach, and was excited about "going from a Bulldog to a Bullet." "Wow," was all she could say. "What are you going to do?"

"Probably work with my dad. Try to save some money."

"You can't get a student loan?"

"I asked about that. Dad says he already borrowed a lot for the business. He said there's no 'equity' left, whatever that means. He said our house is 'underwater.' I don't understand most of this stuff, Liz. I just understand I'm not going to college next year."

Liz fell silent as she considered Chris's situation. There had to be another way.

"What about other schools?" she asked. "Ramapo's got to be cheaper than Gettysburg." Liz's heart jumped at the prospect of Chris attending college with her. "My parents crossed a lot of schools off my list 'cause they were too expensive. I'm paying a lot of my tuition from what I earn at Williamson's."

"Yeah, but you've worked there a couple of years. While I was doing sports, you were making money. I've got a lot of catching up to do....Man, I never expected anything like this would happen."

He ...   **[Deleted]**
              ... route –
              Emily Dickinson, from No. 1150 Lines 7-8

34

"That's the last of it," Michael said, as he rolled his dolly out of the walk-in refrigerator.

"Okay, thanks," the restaurant manager answered. He was a very nervous man, constantly looking about when he met with Michael outside—which was rarely. Usually Michael was ushered into the rear of the restaurant after he knocked, and all business was conducted there. Even then, the manager spoke in hushed tones, often nodding or shaking his head if he could respond that way rather than speaking.

He held the franchise of a nationally renowned steak house chain, an account Michael was surprised to land. "We can only get our meat from company warehouses," the manager had explained when Michael had approached him weeks ago. Then the manager had ushered Michael back out the door less than a minute after he had been admitted. But a few weeks later, the tall, nervous man with the black-framed glasses had approached Michael as he made a delivery at a nearby restaurant. "Can we do business on a strictly confidential, cash-only basis?" he had asked.

"That's the *only* way we can do business," Michael had answered.

Now, twice a week, Michael was stacking cartons of his meats in the chiller next to boxes that carried the chain's logo. Obviously the manager was doing an end-run around the franchise agreement, cutting a corner as so many were doing in these difficult times.

Michael stepped outside and turned to be sure the door locked behind him. Everything went dark. A huge forearm came across his eyes, drawing his head backward and nearly tipping him off his feet. Michael tried to resist. He kicked his legs in all directions. He tried to squirm out of the huge man's grasp. His resistance was stopped suddenly by the awful thrust to the gut, a punch so powerful it sucked away his breath. Michael folded in half as he struggled to begin breathing again. Another blow followed, this to the rib cage. Then another in the same place, and he was stunned with bruising pain. At last, air returned to his lungs, as he struggled with every breath. He was being dragged away, the arm never leaving his eyes even as it crushed against his nose.

Brightness now, as his eyes could again see. The back of his skull slammed against the box of the truck with a solid thud. Marv stood in front of him, his black-gloved hands clenched before him. Michael glanced sideways to see Marv's nameless companion standing ready to rejoin the attack. Michael struggled to retain his balance and resume normal breathing.

"What's the idea of stealing from us?" Marv demanded.

Still stunned, Michael stared blankly at Marv.

Marv delivered another punch to Michael's kidney. "I said, what's the idea of stealing from us?"

"What are you talking about?" Michael countered, eager to stop the blows.

The big man's hand slammed against Michael's forehead, driving his head against the truck again. A shake of Marvin's head and the big man stepped back to his stand-by position.

"We see what you pick up from Rudy. We got the packing house with us now, too. You didn't pay us our full share." Marv stepped forward and extracted the roll of bills from the pocket of

Michael's jeans. He stripped off a few bills and returned the roll.

Michael now sensed how much it hurt to breathe. Talking was not any easier. He considered how much each word of his answer would pain him, even as he came to suspect the source of this disagreement. "Pork—some of it was bad. Couldn't sell it. Had to throw it out."

"You sure you weren't just being cute? Trying to see what you could get away with?"

"No. The pork… was awful. Stunk up… my truck. Had to shitcan it."

"You saying Rudy gave you shitty meat?"

"No. It wasn't selling. I had it for several days before it turned."

Marv considered this for a moment. Then he stepped forward and put his arm around Michael's shoulder. Michael grimaced with pain. A series of coughs followed, as much in revulsion to Marv's suggestion of friendliness as an involuntary effort to return his breathing to normal.

"You see, Michael," Marv whispered into his ear, "we still aren't acting like partners, here. We need to communicate better. You got bad meat—you gotta tell us! Now, you saw how I communicated today, right? Did you understand my message?"

"Yeah," Michael said, even still attempting to protest despite the odds he faced.

"That's the difference. I communicate. You keep things to yourself. You gotta become a member of the team. Tell us your problems. We can be understanding. If you keep quiet, we think you're hiding something from us. Then we get suspicious. And angry. Understand?"

Michael nodded his head.

"Now get back to your route. If what you told us is true, you've got a loss to cover."

Michael watched them walk away and enter their car. He retrieved his dolly and tossed it into the truck and closed up the rear doors. Each of these acts were painful, but they were nothing compared to the pain he felt climbing into the cab. Again he coughed several times as he started the truck's engine. As Marv and his friend drove out of the alley, Michael turned on the radio in the truck.

"...Dow Jones average is down sixty points at this hour. The Justice Department today announced a major crack down on violators of wage and price controls imposed by the Benson administration last year. Attorney General Andrew Watson held a press conference earlier: 'The only way the American People can experience the fairness that Wage and Price Controls offer is if they are uniformly adopted and applied.'"

The difference between Despair
And Fear – is like the One
Between the instant of a Wreck –
And when the Wreck has been –
Emily Dickinson, from No. 305

35

Paul lay quietly in Justin's arms, watching him sleep. He was so much like a boy when they were together like this. Earlier, he had acted much older when he had listened to Paul's recount of his day in Newark.

"I totally lost control, Justin. I split open his head, and pounded him over and over with the butt of my rifle. I think I would have killed him if Stearns hadn't stopped me. It's like I was a killer."

"He had a gun on you, man. Maybe *he* was a killer? You just acted to protect yourself."

"I'm okay with stopping him. But why couldn't I stop myself?"

"Probably adrenaline. Once you get it flowing, it's hard to stop its effect."

"No. There was something more. And I've been feeling it more and more, lately. A feeling of helplessness. A feeling like no matter what I do, it's not going to matter. That this whole crappy world is going to continue to get worse, no matter what I do. I joined the Guard thinking I could make a difference, do some good. But the first time I'm faced with a confrontation, I beat the shit out of some guy with my rifle....It's like my uncle said, I'm just a servant of the State, and it's so easy to become a servant of an out-of-control government."

"There you go again with your paranoia," Justin had said. "The government's not out of control.

The reactionaries were out of control. That's why Benson imposed martial law. To protect the rest of us."

"Reactionaries. Such as...?"

"Landers for one. Remember him? He called for repeal of the Civil Union Act."

"Actually, he said he'd sign it if Congress passed it. It was not really part of his platform."

"That's not what you said at the time. You said he was 'wrong, wrong, wrong!'"

"I did say that," Paul admitted, "on that one issue. But I'm beginning to think he was right about price controls. The inflation he predicted has certainly happened. So prices don't go up—at least not without the government allowing them to—but our wages don't go up either. And the shortages! Who cares if the price stays the same, if there's none of it to buy? That thing they talked about on *Sixty Minutes* last week—remember? How people were driving into Canada to buy what wasn't available here. And how a black market was developing for all kinds of things, because they cost more in Canada and people were willing to pay more here?"

"Look, I don't know anything about economics," Justin had answered. "But I gotta believe the government knows what it's doing."

"Oh, yeah? They've identified four different 'recessions' over the last few years, but I haven't really seen one recovery. One of the guys we busted today—he said he hadn't had a job since 2006. That's ten years! Now it's not right to break into stores in the night and loot. But you should see the frustration on these people's faces. Parts of this country are ready to boil over. That's what I see in Newark. And a guy in our unit told me he saw some intel of similar riots around the country—riots that aren't being reported."

"I don't' know, Paul. You're starting to sound like a reactionary." Are you ready to go back to the way things were before Benson, before they passed the Civil Union Act?"

"Hmmf. What has that really changed? You think I can dare mention you to anyone in my unit?"

Justin had looked at Paul with a curious expression on his face. "Are you saying I'm your little secret?"

And Paul knew that he was helpless. Helpless to deny Justin's charms, regardless of, no, perhaps *because* of, his natural naïveté. Helpless to deny his love for this blond-haired specimen of physical beauty. And helpless to avoid returning tomorrow to the shadows of the underbelly of American society.

We ... **[Deleted]**
... see
Emily Dickinson, from No. 795 Lines 9-10

36

Russell sat in the dark Subaru, his driver's window cracked open about an inch, admitting both the cool night air and whatever sounds were to be heard on this quiet Paterson street. He pulled his coat closed around his neck, feeling under the coat at the same time with his right hand for the comfort the Glock's knurled handle offered. So this is what a stakeout felt like. Cold. Dark. Lonely.

On the seat beside him was an open notebook with a ballpoint pen lying ready on top of it. He had only written the date at the top of the page. There was nothing else to record. Nothing had happened. Three hours of nothing.

Downs had been right. This would be a costly and probably unproductive pursuit for a private investigator.

So Russell was taking a crack at it. Fulfilling, in some bizarre way, an obligation he felt he owed Meredith. An obligation to gather what information he did not know, and do with it he knew not what.

Headlights appeared in the rear view mirror, and Russell slumped in the seat. The car passed, and Russell's heart jumped to his throat. It was a police cruiser. How could he explain himself—sitting here in the dark, miles from his Parsippany home, and carrying an unregistered pistol? Not to mention not having a carry permit.

The patrol car continued down the street, and Russell sighed with relief. His was just another parked car. Nothing to worry about. Nothing to notice.

He shivered a little, and turned on his AM radio to break the emptiness. Then he immediately turned it off. He must stay alert. Must be able to hear any sound. He owed that to Meredith. He owed so much more than that.

Again headlights from the rear, and again, Russell's nerves were alert. This time the car stopped, directly in front of 139 Regiment Street, the residence of Alberto Gonzalez. Two men got out of the car, and Russell could hear them laughing. One was a very large man, somewhat slovenly dressed, an open overcoat revealing shirt and pants straining in their attempt to cover so much flesh with so little cloth. One was as athletic as the other was clumsy, as trim and fit as his friend was overweight. The thin one, Russell suspected, was Gonzalez.

The agile man walked confidently up the steps to the lawn retained above the sidewalk by a whitewashed wall. The other man followed, climbing the steps with effort, pulling himself up using the wrought iron railing. The car continued down the street, turning at the next cross street. Russell jotted down the license plate number, FGO-749. The men entered the house, the door closed, a light came on in a front window. And all was quiet again.

That was it? Three hours for that? Russell glanced at his watch: 9:43. He jotted this trivia onto his pad.

He saw headlights bouncing down the alley behind Gonzalez's house. They stopped and were extinguished near the rear. He heard another car door slam, and very faintly, the sound of a house door opening and closing.

For two more hours, Russell stood vigil. When the light in the window went out, Russell, now slightly chilled, drove around the block, down the alley, and past the large Mercury parked behind the house. He verified the license plate number, then turned for home.

The news station on the radio reported a distillation of the day's major news stories. "Heavy fighting again in the Middle East, as Syrian forces launched hundreds of missiles at Israeli targets. United States and Israeli fighters retaliated with numerous strikes in the Golan Heights and on both sides of the Syrian border...."

I reason, Earth is short –
And Anguish – absolute –
					Emily Dickinson, from No. 301

37

Michael stepped out of the shower and began to gingerly towel off. Green and purple splotches decorated his chest and stomach. He had masked his pain rather well when he had climbed into bed last night, but he had been unable to stop from trembling when Linda had hugged him when she came home earlier. "It's nothing," he had said, as he used his smile to mask the grimace when she hugged him a second time.

Suddenly, Linda was before him again. "Forgot my—*what happened to you*?" she cried.

"Nothing."

"Nothing? You're black and blue! How'd you get those bruises?"

Michael turned away and said nothing. Linda followed around.

"Michael?"

"Linda, please. I'll be okay."

"Did Alberto's men do this?"

Resigned, Michael held Linda to him. "Yes. They thought I was holding out on them. Turns out it was an accounting discrepancy. It shouldn't happen again."

"Michael this isn't right. They can't hurt you like that!"

"Oh yes, they can," Michael countered, moving away from her. "It's quite obvious, they can."

"Can't you do something?"

"Like what? Fight back? Call the police? What do you suggest, Lin?"

"I don't know. But this—this isn't right!"

"Welcome to the underworld," Michael said, as he slipped into his shirt, attempting not to put any pressure on his injuries. "Welcome to my life."

I ...
[Deleted]
... parade –
Emily Dickinson, from No. 405 Lines 9-11

38

Russell jumped when the phone rang. He collapsed back onto his pillow as he realized where he was. Bright sun was streaming in through his bedroom window. He had no early classes today. Rufus, ever loyal, was rising from his spot on the floor next to the bed. The phone rang again, more emphatically it seemed.

"Hello, Dad."

"Karen? Karen, hi! How are you?"

"Uh, that's the thing, Dad. I broke my ankle."

"Broke it? How?"

"The most stupid way possible. I missed a step climbing out of my Eagle. Seven feet down. Landed wrong. Broke it real good."

"Oh, baby!"

"Good news is: I'll be coming home. Probably a few more days here in Tel Aviv, then I'll be grabbing the first available transport back to the States. Should be home for Christmas!"

"That's great, honey. Not that you're hurt, but that you're coming home."

"Yeah. It's great."

To ... ***[Deleted]***
         ... surprise
         Emily Dickinson, from No. 1699 Lines 1-2

39

Russell held the door to Dunkin' Donuts open for a man and a boy, both dressed in ski caps and quilted down coats. The two smiled, and the man thanked him. They appeared to be ready to share a sunny, if brisk, Saturday, enjoying precious weekend time with each other. Russell envied their togetherness and their sense of purpose. He moved quickly to his car to escape the cold.

He started the car and rubbed his hands together, noting with disappointment that the heat gauge had not moved off the "C" limit in the short drive from his house to the donut shop. Soon the car was motoring east on Route 46 and accelerating up the ramp to Interstate 80. When at last the gauge needle moved upward, Russell cranked the heat fan to the maximum setting and was pleased to feel the heat blow from the vents. That made him feel better.

But only a little. Although discouraged by his first stakeout attempt, he was again Paterson-bound for a broad daylight, Saturday morning surveillance. About this he had additional misgivings. He would be more obvious, of course, sitting in a parked car in the daytime. He realized that it wasn't just Alberto and his people that posed a threat, should he be discovered acting suspiciously. Anybody finding his behavior strange enough to alert the authorities would almost be as bad, for he had not been able to devise a reasonable excuse why he, an English professor living in Parsippany, might have a legitimate purpose sitting alone on a street in a mixed neighborhood in Paterson.

Which is why he had done some homework and some preparation. On the seat beside him was a pair of field glasses—Meredith's, from the days when she would seek relaxation and some exercise hiking the woods, fields, and marshes to bird watch. Russell smiled as he remembered how he had teased her about joining her fellow "birders"—"white-haired old ladies in tennis shoes," he had said.

"Most of them are younger than me," she had answered. "Including the guys." She had winked at him as she said that. "You should join me; walk off some of those pounds you've been putting on," she added, patting Russell's "love handles."

Russell grimaced as he unconsciously felt his midriff with one hand. He hadn't been eating right since Meredith was killed, and he had hardly exercised at all. But the paunch of a few months ago was gone, replaced by the gaunt, skeletal frame of a man who slept little and ate even less. A man whose idle moments were filled with unsettling thoughts and nervous energy. A man driven to arm himself against unseen enemies and to stalk someone on the basis of an anonymous phone call.

As for homework, Russell had found on a map a small park on a hill above Alberto's street. From that park Russell believed he might be able to observe secretly without raising much suspicion.

Russell drove slowly down the one-way alley behind Alberto's house, trying not to look at the dark brown Mercury, He was relieved to see it in the same place he had seen it a few nights before. He made his way back to the street, then followed the winding drive that led to the hillside park. Russell parked in a small parking lot adjacent to the drive. Straight out the windshield was a panoramic view of Paterson, including the dark bronzed dome of the county courthouse, the square Spanish-style tower of city hall, the spires of St. Michael's Church and the Cathedral of St. John the Baptist. And right below were the street in front of Alberto's house and the alley in the rear. A quick look through the binoculars confirmed what Russell had hoped: that the park offered an ideal post from which to observe the comings and goings of Alberto Gonzalez.

Russell took a sip of the coffee, still pleasantly hot but now cool enough to drink. He settled himself in the seat and tried to get comfortable. This might turn into another long wait. He had the park to himself. There was little, it seemed to him, to draw anyone to this park on a crisp fall morning. The sun was bright, and might even warm up the day a bit. The Paterson he always pictured as gloomy appeared to shine today, with even its few leafless trees softening the scene. He turned on the radio to break the silence.

"…disappointing sales figures for the third Black Friday in a row. Other merchants reported an up-tick in sales, a much needed boost to an otherwise dismal quarter, but the universal complaint is that the Friday after Thanksgiving—traditionally the busiest shopping day of the year and the kick-off to the Christmas shopping season—again failed to live up to expectations or the enthusiasm consumers exhibited just a few years ago. Wal-mart once again led all merchandisers in sales, and reported growth again this year, based on what they describe as their appeal to price-conscious shoppers."

Russell pressed the tuning button several times in search of another channel, settling at last on an "Oldies" station. It was playing "Open Arms," which had been the song that Meredith and he had danced to at their wedding. He felt a chill as the song gave him the sensation that Meredith was sitting close to him, cuddling for warmth. He remembered dancing to that song. He relived the sensation of turning, turning, the darkened ballroom serving as the universe in which the twin planets—Meredith and he—orbited about each other. In the alternating brightness and darkness of the spotlight, the faces of family and friends surrounding them whirled by like a nearby Milky Way.

He remembered looking at her face, aware— as he had been so many times before, but much more forcefully this time, much more clearly—aware that Meredith's face, her mind, her spirit, all together, they combined to be the perfect match for him. Aware that he was smiling the smile of satisfaction, of completion, of contentment. Aware that she saw his smile as he saw hers, as testament to mutual agreement, united determination, and simple, unquestionable love.

A movement far below caught Russell's attention, and he quickly brought the binoculars to his eyes. A heavy man, wearing an overcoat and a broad-brimmed hat, was standing at Alberto's back door. The man looked up and down the alley, then held the door open for a second man. He was trim and agile and wore an olive trench coat. He was hatless, and Russell felt a rush of excitement, as he recognized him as Gonzalez.

The two descended the steps and moved towards the Mercury, and Russell started his car. Gonzalez seated himself in the passenger seat while the large man took the wheel, although with considerable maneuvering and adjustment to correctly position his mass. Russell backed out of his parking spot and headed down the hill.

Russell reached the point where the alley joined the street just after the Mercury turned towards downtown. He backed off so as to allow the Forester to follow several car lengths behind. Left and right the Mercury turned, making its way down the residential streets. Russell dropped back even further, keeping a full city block separation, often seeing his quarry make a right turn before he made his left. At last they turned onto Market Street, and Russell was able to close the distance as he blended in with the traffic. At one traffic light Russell was right behind them, and he brought his car to a stop just two feet away. Then he lay back again, allowing a service van pulling out from a side street to fall in between them.

A few more turns and Russell was again snaking through a residential neighborhood, again keeping a discreet distance. At last the Mercury pulled to the curb next to a public school. Russell drove on past, being careful to stare straight ahead, just as he had seen it done in undercover cop movies. In his rear view mirror he saw the two men exit the car and pass through a gate into the paved playground. Russell rounded the corner and parked. His vantage point provided a complete view of the playground. The neighborhood was quiet. No one walked the sidewalks. No cars moved on the streets.

Russell could see Alberto walking alongside the school building, his overweight companion struggling to keep the pace. Scanning ahead, Russell saw three men in the far corner. He grabbed his binoculars for a better look. A burly man in a long black coat was holding another against the chain link fence. The second man was underdressed for the cold, wearing just a sweater. He also appeared distressed, and Russell could see bright red blood flowing from his nose. The third man, also in a black coat, but much thinner, was looking about nervously.

This was real street violence, and Russell was a witness to it. The news reports constantly described it, but through his own eyes it was now more vivid.

When Gonzalez and his companion approached, the man in the sweater became more agitated, and the burly man had to struggle a little to contain him. Once there, Gonzalez's heavy driver relieved the burly man. He grasped the victim by the throat rather than the shoulder. The burly man and his thin partner stepped away and began to survey the neighborhood. Although seventy-five yards away, Russell dropped his binoculars and slumped down in his seat to avoid detection. He hoped they hadn't spotted him. He was ready to race off if they had.

With his unaided eyes, Russell watched as Gonzalez approached the man. Their heads were very close, and even from this distance Russell felt the victim's terror. The large man lifted the victim off his feet which began to flail as he did so. Gonzalez stepped even closer, as if to whisper in the victim's ear. Then began the assault, as Gonzalez delivered a salvo of blows to the victim's torso, and a final, powerful blow to the head. The heavy man let go, and the victim collapsed to the ground. Gonzalez kicked the victim forcefully two times. Then he leaned over him as if to deliver a final message. Gonzalez conferred briefly with the thin man before the four of them walked back to their cars, the victim left lying motionless beneath a basketball goal.

Russell slumped deeper into his seat as the two vehicles started. Gonzalez's Mercury swept a wide u-turn in the intersection behind him, while the second car, a black Ford with the burly man driving, turned and drove past him. Russell made a note of the license plate, jotting it down in his notebook after the car turned out of sight.

Russell looked back at the scene of the assault where the man continued to lie still. Russell jumped out of the car, opened his trunk, and grabbed a wool Army surplus blanket he kept there. He then jogged along the fenced playground to the gate and rushed forward to where the man lay.

Kneeling down by the man, Russell gently rocked his shoulder. He appeared to be barely conscious. Russell was relieved to hear a low moan, and the man brought his arms up as if would try to push himself up.

"Hey, not so fast, there," Russell said, spreading the blanket over him. "I'm going to call an ambulance. You lay here and try not to move."

"No!" the man answered.

Russell was surprised by the man's insistence, even more so when he rose up on an elbow and pleadingly turned his face towards him. Blood covered much of his face. It had crusted between his nose and mouth, but was still flowing from a cut above his eye and from his swelling lips.

"You're hurt bad," Russell made his own plea. "Let me get you some help."

"No!" he again responded, punctuating his refusal with a labored cough. "No ambulance. No police." He grimaced. "I need to get home."

The man struggled to rise further, wobbling on his elbow, his face distorted with a grimace of pain. Russell felt he should argue, but had little confidence of success based on the reaction so far.

"You're sure?"

"Yes...just need to get home."

"I'll take you, then," Russell said, a little surprised with himself that he was acquiescing. "Here, let me help you up."

For a rather small man, he seemed like a large weight on Russell's shoulder. Only by getting his legs under the man was Russell able to raise him to his feet. Once upright, the man steadied himself, but continued to lean heavily on his aide. Then he turned towards Russell, and painfully squeezed out a question.

"Who...who are you?"

"I was just passing by. Saw you get beat up from a distance. I really think you should get some medical attention."

The man shook his head, and Russell gave up.

"You think you can walk some?"

"Yeah," the man wheezed. Russell looked around quickly for any sign the attackers had returned.

Russell led the victim along the school

building, pausing several times to allow him to catch his breath in desperate gasps interrupted with painful coughs. When they reached the gate, Russell leaned him against the fence.

"I'm going to get my car. It'll take a few minutes. You stay here, okay?"

"Yes….and thanks."

"Yeah," Russell said, watching him as he backed away until he was confident the man could stand. Then he turned and jogged back to fetch his car. He drove around the block, pulling to the curb next to the gate, slightly surprised that the man had waited for him. Then again, how far could he have gone? Russell helped the man to the car, and eased him into the passenger seat, clearly a painful endeavor.

"Where to?" Russell asked as he slipped in behind the wheel.

"Turn left there," the man said, pointing weakly towards the next intersection.

As they twisted through the neighborhood, Russell said nothing, and the man to his right spoke only to give directions. It was clear that his passenger wished to reveal nothing, and Russell did not wish to reveal anything about himself, either. Certainly he did not wish to make known that he was following Gonzalez or that he even knew who he was. It made for a surreal journey.

At last the rider directed Russell to pull to the curb, and like a dedicated chauffeur, Russell hustled around the car and helped the man to his feet. Together they crossed the sidewalk to a nondescript door that appeared to lead to an apartment in the rear of a Chinese Restaurant fronting a cross street. As he squeezed through the door, he shifted his weight off Russell and onto the door jam, and turned to face his benefactor.

"Thank you….thank you, whoever you are."

The door closed, and Russell was left to ponder those words.

Love ...   ***[Deleted]***   *... longer*
Emily Dickinson, from No. 491 Line 7

40

    Liz stood at the display table, re-folding the sweaters. It was amazing how so few customers could make such a mess of a display. She had already put the display back together first thing that morning, undoing the damage of Black Friday. It had been a long day in the store, but she was energized today, perhaps now more aware than ever before, how fleeting economic security can be. She worked almost automatically, the garments falling into conformity with just a few hand movements and hardly any brain involvement. That was good, because her mind was on other things.

    Her parents for one. She had heard them arguing after her doctor's appointment. Well, not really arguing. Dad was ranting, and Mom was trying to calm him down. Again. She was the glue that held the family together. If only Elmer's could put it in a bottle.

    Liz knew things were tough. She didn't need news reports—which she seldom listened to—she had her Dad, an extremely sensitive barometer for measuring all kinds of pressures. Since he'd bought the meat truck, he seemed more touchy than usual, a glass vase on the edge of a table ready to crash to the floor with the slightest vibration.

    A good example was his reaction when Chris and she had cut class. Such a big deal! He had no clue how their infraction paled in comparison to what happened everyday at Garfield High. The fights, the weapons, the talking back, disrespect, bullying, vandalism—Chris and she were model students against that backdrop. Mr. Barnes had probably forgotten all about the incident, he had so many other things to worry about.

And Mom should have known better. Heck, things were probably worse at Wallington, where she worked. But she joined right in, backing up Dad's stern ruling. A real united front. Liz had hoped she might ask for a reduction in sentence. It had been several weeks, and she had behaved herself. For the most part. But she needed the right conditions to make the request, the right atmosphere in which to send up the trial balloon. With Dad stressed out, and Mom all tense, this wasn't the time.

A vibration in her hip pocket alerted her to an incoming text message. She glanced over at Marci. She looked to be totally absorbed by her store status report. Liz slipped her cell phone out of her pocket and snuggled it between two sweaters on the table.

CHRIS: u busy?

Another peek at Marci, then Liz's thumbs attacked the tiny keyboard.

LIZ: work whasup?
CHRIS: Tx 4 wed glad u there 4 me
LIZ: no prob
CHRIS: dad trying 2 find $ 4 college not sure he can he & uncle phil r tight
Liz: so sorry it really sucks

Liz looked up to see Marci putting away her paperwork. She turned to her phone one more time.

LIZ: got 2 go luv u

Liz slid the phone into her pocket and moved to the suits. She began straightening the garments and sorting the hangers by size.

The dashing of Chris's college plans did suck. Chris had told her that his uncle had lost his job through no fault of his own. Something about a change in government regulations had put his whole division out of business. Phil's son, Chris's cousin, had lost his college money a year earlier, too. The house couldn't be sold in this market, and as Chris had said, "My whole family, Dad and Uncle Phil, they're too proud to just walk away from their obligations."

Somehow, this trouble seemed to bring Chris and Liz even closer together. When he hugged her now, she felt more of a squeeze, but, in a strange way, more tenderness, too. She knew for sure that she loved him, and that she always would. And in light of that knowledge, nothing else mattered.

I ...   *[Deleted]*
         ... come –
            Emily Dickinson, from No. 51 Lines 5-6

41

Rufus's nose went to work, sniffing the blanket that Russell carried into the house. Russell anxiously recalled that blood-born pathogens could be deadly, and tried to remember everywhere he had touched the man beaten so badly on the playground. Had he come in contact with any of his blood? He carefully placed the blanket in the washing machine, and spun the dial to "Heavy."

He had certainly lost no time in learning about Gonzalez. He was a brutal thug, willing to pick up where his soldiers left off. Indeed, he seemed to relish the delivery of his brutality, making it part of his personal message. Russell had no problem imagining Gonzalez carrying out a savage murder, and his whole body began to shake as he conjectured that the monster might even have enjoyed pumping two slugs into Meredith's chest.

If Russell were to continue these surveillance operations—and he had every intention of doing so—what should he do if something like today's episode started to play out? Gonzalez had already played one "Get Out of Jail Card." The Voice had suggested and Lance Bloom had confirmed he might very well have more to use. How practical, then, was it to call the authorities, even if they were close enough to respond in time? On the other hand, what could he do, alone, outnumbered four to one? No doubt pistols were underneath those overcoats he saw today. Russell would be a marked—and easily located—man, should any of the goons get away.

Russell drew the Glock from his shoulder holster and examined it. *Was this what it had come down to—every man for himself, the law of the jungle, force trumping laws? Was his teaching Elizabethan English just a flimsy sham, a barely translucent veil to mask the lawlessness and the inhumanity of the times?*

Rufus nuzzled his hand to get attention. Russell holstered the gun and pet his friend. Rufus was the one constant in his life, the sole holdover from the happier days. Russell remembered their trips together, the three of them, the dog serving as only the obvious excuse for seeking out an empty field or a quiet woodland trail. Returns to such places had been disappointing. He never seemed to be able to fill the void the absence of his wife had created. Even Rufus seemed to miss her. As if he feared another tragic separation, the dog no longer romped ahead down the path nor charged exuberantly into the field, flushing out all kinds of birds and mammals. Instead, he stayed close to his master's side. When Russell was absent for long periods, the dog sometimes destroyed things by chewing. The chewed tassel on Russell's loafer was a mild example compared to the pair of shoes the dog totally destroyed.

Russell feared that the same loss of spirit was infecting his own life. He was listless around the house, and the list of things that needed to be done had grown to two pages. That he even wrote them down caused him to consider himself especially dedicated. But to actually do the work? He had no inclination whatsoever. He tried—he really did—to maintain enthusiasm for his teaching, if nothing else. But he had felt the lapses in his lectures, the shortage of passion, and the blank looks his students returned in his direction.

Only Alberto Gonzalez was worthy of his interest. Russell could focus on no other subject so intently. He expected that more and more of his free time would be devoted to watching Gonzalez, and he didn't care. Indeed, he looked forward to the next stakeout. He looked forward to watching from the outside, trying to learn as much as he could about the man, his associates, and his organization. He imagined he was a lion, moving slowly through the tall grass, getting closer and closer to the zebra until the time was right to strike. No, not a lion. His actions did not seem kingly. They were not so directed. The outcome was not so certain. No, he was more like a praying mantis. Waiting. Watching. Blending in. Assuming a reverent stance even as he sat ready to deliver violent, unholy justice.

*Drowning is not so pitiful
As the attempt to rise*

Emily Dickinson, from No. 1718

42

"Hey, Rudy," Michael said, grabbing the butcher's meaty hand in a firm handshake. Rudy had just wiped his mitt before offering it to him, but Michael could always feel the fatty slipperiness that stayed behind. "Can we talk?"

"Yeah, sure, Mike," Rudy said, leading him away from the cutting table toward the small office in the corner of the plant.

"Listen," Michael said, looking around surreptitiously for eavesdroppers, "I was wondering if we could do a little extra business—off the books."

Rudy looked around to assure himself the other meat cutters' attention was focused on their tables. "I don't know, Mike. You know Alberto's got his hands in the operation, now. Things aren't the same."

"Tell me about it. I was doin' okay, before. But now, it's tough. I've got a truck payment due, and I'm not sure how I'm goin' to make it." Michael shivered slightly. Even wearing his coat, he felt cold in here. He always did. He never understood how Rudy could stand it, and in short sleeves, no less.

"Yeah, things are tough all over. I went to the owners when Alberto tried to muscle in," Rudy said. "They told me it was my problem. That I should handle it. They give me a lot of control here. But they expect me to cover their asses, too. But hey, I got no experience with that kind of thing. I'm a lover, not a fighter! So I tell Alberto's goon to shove off. Three days in a row, I come outta here and one of my car tires is slashed—the third day, right under the noses of the cops! The owners would have a cow if they knew I called the police, but I had to do something—a tire a day? So even with the cops keepin' an eye out for me, they got to me. Maybe they own the cops, too, I don't know. Anyway, I couldn't afford it. So I jack up the price a little, and now I survive."

"Yeah, the restaurants squealed when the price went up," Michael acknowledged, "but what choice do they have? I saw pictures on the 'net of feed lots out in Colorado: the cattle just shot and left to rot. 'Too expensive to feed them,' they said. Especially after the grain suppliers got an exemption from *their* price controls. The whole world's screwed up, Rudy."

"Right. And you want to screw it up some more?"

"Not much. Nothing to make Alberto question anything, no change to his activity. I'm just asking to buy more, on a separate account, something I can resell without Alberto bein' the wiser. How does he know what you're bringin' in?"

"He doesn't. At least not yet. He's dyin' to find out, though. The owners'll keep him out of here, physically at least—they draw the line there. But he learns by observing. I see his gorillas watching this place all the time."

"Rudy, I wouldn't ask this if I didn't have to. But I'm just squeezed too thin. If you could give me just a few more packages a week. I promise you, I'll be careful. This won't come back to haunt you." Michael studied the butcher's eyes. He hated to put him in this position, but he had little choice. Profits were slim before Alberto started taking his cut. His family was already leaning on Linda's earnings more than he wished. His wife spent her time on the computer, printing out coupons. She never went to the store without them. He also noticed that she never shopped for herself, anymore. Food, his occasional need, and whatever Liz needed that she didn't buy herself at Williamson's at discount—that was all Linda spent money on. Everything else had gone to pay off the truck or into Liz's college account.

Alberto could lend him some money, of course. But he was already too involved with him. Seeking out a second black market source was extremely risky. And the logistics of making another pickup stop every day wouldn't be missed by Alberto for long.

"I don't know, Mike. I gotta protect the owners and keep Alberto in the dark, all to keep my own ass out of a sling."

'Rudy—please? The owners'll get extra volume. It's just Alberto we gotta watch."

Rudy looked at him, looked away, and then looked back. "We go back a long way, Michael. Back to when you opened that deli in Lodi." Rudy exhaled heavily, before continuing. "All right. But be careful. There'll be hell to pay if Alberto gets wind of this."

The ...   *[Deleted]*   ... *bride*
Emily Dickinson, from No. 1 Line 21

43

The wind pressed hard against the Forester's door, and Russell pushed harder to open it. Overhead, sooty clouds churned, and little white plumes spilled down below before boiling up and away. Russell pulled his overcoat closed, fastening two buttons. He leaned into the wind as he walked through the gate into the dreary graveyard.

It had been such a bright place on the day they had laid Meredith to rest. The granite tombstones had glistened in the sunshine, rising out of the cool grass to affirm their timelessness and appearing so resolute in their stand against eternity.

Today, the grave markers appeared smaller, as if they were being squashed by the low-lying clouds and being pressed into the cold dark soil beneath some giant thumb. The grass, too, was no longer vibrant, but wore the dark green of the winter season, a conservative suit in a bearish season.

To his right, Route 46 traffic streamed by, the occupants of the vehicles hardly aware the cemetery even existed, just beyond the highway's shoulder. Certainly no one took note of him, a short man in his dark overcoat, hunched against the cold and leaning into the wind, striding determinedly through this old, maple-rimmed burial ground. Even with their leaves gone, the surrounding trees shielded—secluded—this hallowed ground.

And what of those that lie below? Below, out of sight, to hide the chemistry, to relieve the grief, and to affirm conclusively the temporal nature of man. Only the cold stone markers provided clues, in clichéd shorthand, of who slept below. Bulky boulders registered, with uniform clumsiness, the dogged longevity or tragic shortfall of lives bounded by two dates. They recorded, in carefully chosen verbiage measured against a cost per letter scale, the utilitarian life of a mason or the futility of a career devoted to the fine arts. They revealed, with pitiable ineptitude, the shreds of severed love and the short-lived promises of faithful remembrance.

Russell approached Meredith's spot, her mound standing higher than the others, the few rains of this autumn having done little to wear it down. Only a few blades of grass found the excavated clay and gravel inviting enough to set down roots. The ferrous-colored soil served to further set her space apart, awaiting erosion, cultivation, and grooming, as if the grave's new occupant were still in the process of settling in.

He knelt by the grave to be closer to Meredith, but he held no illusions of communicating with her, so he did not speak aloud. He did not come here to reunite with her. Their union had been so perfect; its destruction so final. He did not have to come here to feel this. He was aware of it during every waking moment, and sometimes when he slept, too.

He did not come here for peace, either. Somehow, he knew if Meredith were aware of what was going on, she would be more restless than he. Professor Fitzsimmons had just this week published a paper, amidst great fanfare generated by Schuyler's administration, calling for more wage and price controls. He argued that the reason consumer prices were rising were the "loopholes" that allowed certain wholesale prices to rise and permitted such increases to be passed on by retailers.

Russell felt a surge of acidity in his mouth. He was actually sick to his stomach thinking of this. One of Meredith's greatest traits had been her humility.

Never could she conceive that she, some committee of geniuses, or even a super-computer could better devise an economic plan superior to the millions of decisions individuals made in the marketplace each day. That Fitzsimmons or people like him believed they could was a condition that would drive Meredith crazy.

Russell turned toward the highway. He hadn't remembered hearing the cars whiz by during the funeral. Had he been so detached to be that unaware? Now he heard a constant hum of engines, the cyclical braking for the traffic light at Vail Road, the occasional percussive beat of a blasting stereo system. The traffic seemed an intrusion—not because of the noise, but rather the in-your-face contempt the motorists showed by driving on in the routines of their lives past the shattered remains of Russell's.

So why did he come here? Not for peace, certainly, as he turned back towards the grave. Not to commune with Meredith, or her spirit, or even her memory. He did not have to be here to do that. Not for any comfort in a religious sense. The preacher's words at the service—words like grace, reward, home, celebration, rejoicing—had sounded as hollow as the resonations from the clods of earth striking the coffin lid. True, Russell had his faith, such as it was. But it was more of a foundation for living this life than a deed for an eternal retirement community, one for which he had not even seen a slick brochure. And this life had been drastically changed.

There was Karen, of course. But she was grown now: stronger, smarter, and braver than he had ever been. Independent, too. She didn't need him. Even with a broken foot, she was coming home to comfort him more than to seek his aid. He would no doubt be more a liability to her than anything else as the years progressed. Meredith and he—especially Meredith—had done a good job of raising Karen. He was immensely proud of her. And that pride had a place: in a seat in the rear of the auditorium.

His best guess was that he came here out of commitment. A formal commemoration of the life they once shared and the love he still possessed. It was a socially acceptable act of grief and growth, and a personally satisfying attempt at rededication in the neighborhood of hopeless loss.

Russell studied the chrysanthemums he carried. She had always loved these flowers, especially the purple ones. Each year, more and more bunches of the prolific plants appeared in new flower beds, transplanted by Meredith from beds where they were overrunning anything else planted there. Her efforts had provided him with a bountiful supply of autumn blooms to adorn her grave.

He leaned forward to place the flowers on the grave. Before he could weight them down with a few stones, the wind had grabbed one and spirited it away. Russell lunged for it, lost his balance, and fell, landing with his chest atop the mound. He lay there for a moment, stunned by his clumsiness, surprised that the earth did not feel as cold as he would have expected. Recomposing himself, he returned to a kneeling position and put the wayward blossom with the others. He secured them all with a fist-sized stone lying nearby. Then he brushed clean his hands, and with them, attempted to wipe the soil from his coat. It was hopelessly stained. He had then yet another reminder of the loss of Meredith, and a symbolic demonstration of what embracing her memory entailed.

We ... **[Deleted]**
... rise
Emily Dickinson, from No. 1176 Lines 1-2

44

Russell's spot on the hill seemed colder today, despite the sunshine and the clear sky. Maybe it had something to do with the emptiness. Not just the emptiness of the park—only the occasional jogger or dog walker passed by, even on a Saturday morning. It was also the emptiness of Russell's quest: the hours spent sitting in his car, staring down at the small frame house, the only house he cared about in all of Paterson.

Russell was amazed at his own resolve. Nine days in a row he had come up here, made possible by Schuyler's break between semesters. Nine days of sitting in his car, watching the house. Nine days of shivering, as mid-December had been taken hostage by a long cold spell fueled by arctic air sweeping down from Canada. Nine days of drinking coffee and discreetly relieving himself in the bushes along the edge of the ravine. Nine days of nothing to show for his effort, only a few brief sightings of Gonzalez or his henchmen since the day he had witnessed the beating of that hapless victim. Even the briefcase full of final exams he had brought along one day to grade had done little to break the monotony.

Yet still he came. It wasn't an obsession. With the detachment of an academic, he had ruled out that psychological deviation. He didn't wake up each morning with the uncontrollable desire to come here. Rather, he awoke each day to be met by the horror of Meredith's absence. This, in turn, spurred him to reflect on his loss and to honor her memory. And reflection and honor motivated his actions: to learn whatever he could about the man he believed was implicated in her murder.

So when the black Ford pulled up in front of the house and the thin man walked briskly up the walk and entered the house, Russell considered if it might be time for a change in tactics. Gonzalez didn't move much during the day; that had become obvious. He was apparently content to sit inside and conduct his business via telephone or trust his associates to conduct field operations. It occurred to Russell that the men in the black Ford were the movers and shakers. They had initiated the attack on the man who lived behind the Chinese restaurant. Gonzalez had just shown up to provide the *coup de grace.* Perhaps the two mooks in the black sedan could provide more insight into Gonzalez's business.

A cloud of exhaust from the Ford's tailpipe and the fact that the thin man alone had emerged from the passenger side of the car, suggested that it would soon be on the move again. Russell decided that today he would follow it. Sure enough, the man emerged a few minutes later. As he walked back to the car, Russell put his car into motion and began to coast downhill.

Adrenaline raced through his arteries as he followed the Ford through the city. Just as he had done when he had followed Gonzalez, Russell kept his distance, being careful not to pull out too quickly and allowing a city block or more of separation. Within a few minutes, however, the Ford was climbing the ramp onto Route 80 eastbound, and Russell closed the distance in case the driver he was following had a heavy foot.

They traveled into Bergen County, observing the Interstate's speed limit. A few exits later they left the highway, and Russell found himself in Garfield, traversing streets that were somehow familiar to him.

Only when they made the final turn did Russell make the connection. It was the street where the teacher lived, the one he had brought home from Drew. Maybe fifty yards after passing the very house where he had dropped her off, the black Ford pulled to the curb and parked. Russell continued on past, avoiding even glancing at the target as he did so. He drove out of sight, turned around in a driveway, and then doubled back. He found a secluded place to park almost out of sight, but where he could still see the sedan. The binoculars could come in handy here, but Russell was careful not to use them in excess. He did not want to call any attention to himself, slumped behind the wheel while parked at the curb of a quiet residential street.

For more than a half hour they sat; no one in either car moving. Then Russell's eye was grabbed by a movement in the distance. A woman—no, a girl—was walking down the teacher's driveway towards the street. Russell focused the binoculars on the girl while she was still on the drive. It was the teacher's daughter. *What was the girl's name? Garfield High School...graduating next spring...Liz! That was it: Liz.* At the end of the drive she turned toward the corner, away from the sedan and him,

She stopped at the corner and stood there, in no hurry to go further. A few minutes later a bus pulled up along the main road and stopped. Liz stepped aboard. No sooner did the bus pull from the curb, than the sedan made a U-turn, and then made the right turn to follow the bus. Russell stomped on the accelerator to close the distance. All the time wondering what was the connection between Gonzalez's goons and the high school English teacher—*Norton, yes, Linda Norton.*

Saturday morning traffic was beginning to increase. It was nearly nine. The bus lumbered down the thoroughfare, stopping repeatedly for customers. The Ford followed close behind. Farther behind, trying to be as unnoticeable as possible, Russell followed. He had stopped in traffic so as not to close the distance during one of the bus's frequent stops. A few drivers glared at him as they passed. Fortunately no one sounded their horn at him. He prayed that the men in the Ford would not notice him.

The bus turned onto an even busier artery, and soon stopped adjacent to a shopping plaza a full two blocks long. Russell saw Liz climb off the bus and start walking across the parking lot. As the bus pulled away, the Ford turned into the parking lot and soon parked not far from the street, but at a distance from the stores that any shopper would spurn. Russell watched as Liz entered a woman's clothing store and another employee locked the door behind her. He slipped into a parking spot not far away. Most of the stores had not yet opened, and, except for customers at a luncheonette and Starbucks, there was plenty of parking available. From there he kept an eye on the Ford in the distance and the front door of the store. He was conscious that he was unbuttoning his coat and reaching to his belt for the comforting feel of the pistol's grip in his right hand.

Suddenly, he felt his heart racing. The seatbelt was confining, unbearably so. He released it and threw it aside. He had to be ready. Ready to jump out of the car, the Glock freed from its holster, ready to portion out the prescribed dosage of lead in copper cladding so as to protect—*to protect who? (No,* whom! *Objective case, after all.) To protect a girl he had driven home from school, once, more than a month ago.*

This was too weird. Who goes around following teenage girls on sunny Saturday mornings in busy shopping centers? Perhaps...perhaps the same sort of people who assault middle-aged men on school playgrounds. The same sort of people who would gun down an innocent Meredith. Russell was, as Karen would have described it, "on heightened alert."

Thirty minutes passed, with no change in status, except that shoppers had begun to stream into the parking lot and the stores. *What were the two goons waiting for? Why would they delay the confrontation—if there was to be one—until there were more witnesses, more potential victims of collateral damage?* Russell felt his heart sink under a sudden pressure. If he were to use his weapon, to defend Liz or anyone else, he was reminded of the awesome responsibility he would have.

Then the thin man got out of the Ford. *What to do? Confront him in the parking lot? And say—what? "I've been following you, and I think you may be up to no good." No, that won't work.* The thin man was clearly making his way to the store where Liz was. Russell jumped out of his car and hustled inside first.

Where is she? It's not a big store. The display tables weren't that high. A girl as tall as Liz would be seen. There were few customers in the store with whom she could blend. Maybe she's in the back room? Suddenly Liz stood up from behind a table near the rear of the store. He moved hastily in that direction. He was within a few feet of her when he looked over his shoulder to see the thin man enter.

"May I help you—"Liz began to speak with the banality of retailspeak before her voice suddenly changed. "Don't I know— Hey, you...you're the college professor! Remember? You picked me up at school when my mom's car broke down!"

"Oh, yes! How are you?" Russell did not let on that this was anything but an accidental encounter. "You work here?" Russell looked again toward the front of the store. The thin man was walking intently in Liz's direction.

"Yeah. Got to start paying tuition in less than a year!"

"I see." *Thin man was fifteen yards away and closing.* Russell eased the Glock from the holster and

178

held it at belt level inside his coat.

He was an ugly cuss. Tiny bead-like eyes flitted above a crooked nose and a sneering mouth. His facial features appeared to have been stitched together by a less-than competent Dr. Frankenstein. The lapels of a cheap suit were visible inside the trench coat.

"So, are you looking for something in particular?" Liz continued.

"Uh, yes." Russell was answering her, but his eyes were focused on the man. "I was thinking of buying a top for my daughter. She's coming into town in a few days."

"Okay, what size is she?"

Just a few feet away, the thin man began to peruse the racks, but without intent. Russell re-checked the front to be sure thin man's burly partner hadn't followed him in. "I haven't a clue! Typical male shopper, right?"

Liz smiled. Russell was suddenly aware how attractive, how friendly, how decent she was. His resolve to be her protector steeled.

"Yeah, we get that quite often, believe it or not."

Thin man continues to study a rack of cocktail dresses.

"I'd say she's about your size. No, a little taller. An athletic build—like you."

"Well, in that case, why don't you try over here. 'Medium' would probably fit, but you might get a 'Large,' just to be safe. She might gather it with a belt to keep it from looking like a tent, if it's too big. Or, of course, she can always return it."

"Thanks. I'll give them a look."

"You're welcome."

Liz turned toward the thin man, and Russell all but drew the pistol outside his coat.

"May I help you?" she asked. *He didn't even deserve that much greeting.*

"Just looking." His voice was guttural without any refinement. Russell no longer even pretended to be shopping. He was watching the thin man's hands for any sign of aggressive movement.

"Well, let me know if I can help." Liz stepped back to the counter where she was laying out a display.

Another minute and the thin man left without saying another word to anyone. Russell released two lungfuls of charged air, and quietly slipped his pistol back into its holster.

He found an aqua colored top and had Liz box it when he checked out. Through the store window he could see that the Ford was gone.

> *Meeting ...* ***[Deleted]***
> *... design*
> Emily Dickinson, from No. 1548 Lines 1-2

45

There had been many times that he had been made fun of. Even Meredith had taken her turns, teasing him for dwelling in the nineteenth century because he hadn't yet bought a cell phone.

"I really don't need one," he had explained to one of his students. "You'd be surprised how few things in life are truly that urgent in nature."

But he wished he had one now. His attempts to locate a pay phone in Garfield proved fruitless. Apparently the phone company had embraced the twenty-first century as tightly as he had hugged the nineteenth. And the idolizer of Emily Dickinson had never even noticed that phone booths were as passé as buggy whips.

He drove west on Route 80, repeatedly reining in his speed. He didn't need to be stopped by the police. For sure, it seemed he was doing their job already: stakeouts, moving surveillances, interventions. As such, his behavior was as suspicious as the men in the Ford. And that was another problem he would have to resolve by the seat of his pants.

Rufus was certainly confused as Russell rushed into the house and passed him waiting at the door. Reaching his study, Russell scattered the papers from his briefcase before finding the sheet he remembered: the roster from the Drew symposium, complete with phone numbers. He ran to the phone and dialed, then took two deep breaths as he heard it ring. He had to sound absolutely calm, given what he was about to say.

Mrs. Norton answered, and her tempered, grounded voice came forcefully through the receiver. This was in direct opposition to how Russell suspected his voice would sound.

"Mrs. Norton? It's Russell Grayson. From Schuyler University. We met at the symposium at Drew."

"Professor Grayson? This is, uh, a surprise."

"Mrs. Norton, listen to me. It's about Liz."

"Liz, what about Liz?"

"What I am about to tell you will sound bizarre. It will also sound alarming. I do not wish to alarm you, but I feel I must warn you. It's going to sound crazy. I can't change that. I just ask that you believe me that I'm telling you the truth. And also, regardless how unusual this may sound, I again am being truthful and just want to tell you something I know."

"Professor, I—"

"Please. Just hear me out." Russell took another breath and exhaled. He wasn't at all sure he could pull this off. "This morning your daughter caught a bus to her job; she works at a fashion store."

"Yes..."

"Mrs. Norton, your daughter was followed."

"What?"

"Please. She was followed by two men. One tall and thin, another on the heavy side. They drive a black Ford Taurus."

"Wait—"

"I know this, because *I* was following *them*!"

"What?!"

"Stay with me! I don't know their names, but I do know something about them. They are criminals. I have seen them brutally beat a defenseless man."

"I don't understand—why would they follow Liz?

"They followed her to the store, and one of

them, the thin one, went inside. Liz even spoke to him. I know, because I was there. Ask her, she will tell you that I was there and bought an aqua colored woman's top."

"Wait! This is all going too fast. You were following Liz?"

"No! I was following them…following Liz. Listen, I told you this was going to sound strange. You have to believe me. I wish you and your family no harm. But these two men, I don't know what their interest is, but I can't believe it's anything good."

"Liz—she's still at the store?"

"Yes. She was there when I left, about thirty, forty minutes ago. The two men had left before I did."

"And you didn't call the police?"

"No. I can't. For reasons I can't really explain." Russell knew he could not avoid this part of the conversation. "Listen. I have my own reasons for following those two. Reasons that are even stranger than what I've told you already. You call the police. Please, you call them. You can; I can't. That's why I'm telling you. Just— just, please don't mention my name. You have to trust me on that."

A long silence followed. Russell had done his best. He awaited her decision.

"Professor, I…I don't know what to say. This is so unbelievable."

"Mrs. Norton, remember the day your car broke down? Remember how I helped you?"

"Yes, you were very kind."

"I still am trying to be. Believe what I've told you. And be very careful."

If ...   **[Deleted]**
           ... me
   Emily Dickinson, from No. 29 Lines 1-2

46

"Liz?"

"Mom?! You know you shouldn't call me here. They could fire me for talking on my cell on the sales floor."

"Liz, are you all right?"

"Of course, I'm all right. Hey! You know who came in the store today? That professor from Schuyler who gave us a ride home. You remember him?"

Classic Liz. Never let a few employment rules stop her from talking on the phone. Still, it was good to hear her voice. "Yes, honey. But listen to me. Has anyone been in the store today…acting strange?"

"Mom, what are you talking about? It's just another Saturday at Williamson's."

"What about earlier, when the professor was there?"

"Mother! Everything's fine. Nobody—"

Linda's breathing stopped as abruptly as Liz's speech.

"—there was a guy, a creepy looking guy in a black overcoat. He was here when Mr. Grayson was talking to me. But he just looked at some things and then left. Uh, oh! Marci's giving me the eye. I gotta hang up. I'll see you later."

"Liz—"

Michael came into the kitchen from the garage as Linda hung up the phone. "I got the lights you wanted. Can you come out and hold the ladder so I can string 'em up? The temperature's supposed to drop tonight, and I want to get this done. It's cold enough already."

"Mike—"She could tell he was reading her face, and he didn't like the story it told. He was in front of her in an instant, holding her shoulders and fully attentive as to why she might be upset. "I got a call today, from Professor Grayson."

He released her and turned aside. Linda knew this reaction. She knew how his eyes would cloud and the veins in his neck would stretch. How she hated it. Most of the time he appeared to be forty. At times like this he acted like he would soon be four.

"So, he's back, is he?"

"Michael, stop it—"

"'Just a ride home, that's all.'"

"Michael, listen to me." Linda grabbed his shoulder and wheeled him around to face her. "Someone followed Liz to work today."

"What are you saying?"

"Someone followed Liz to work today!"

"Who?"

"Two men. Possibly criminals."

"We need to call Liz."

"I just did. She sounds all right. The men have left."

"Who were they?"

"Two men driving a black Taurus watched Liz get on the bus and followed her to Williamson's. One of them even went into the store!"

Michael had stopped his tantrum as fast as it had started. With this news he appeared stunned. "Shit," was all he said.

"Mike? What's wrong?"

"Two men. One fat and one skinny?"

"Why, yes. Wearing—"

"—black overcoats," he said, finishing her sentence. "It's Alberto's men."

"Alberto? But why?"

"I don't know, but I'm going to find out on Monday."

"I don't like this," Linda said. "What possible reason would they have to follow Liz? Are these the two that attacked you?"

Michael nodded silently, and Linda could see his eyes were focused on some plan to be hatched in two days.

"Mike, I don't think you should confront them. We need to call the police."

"Really, Linda?" His mind was back in the room with her. "'Yes, officer, these two mobsters my husband works with in his black market job followed my daughter, and I want them arrested.' How is that going to play, Lin?"

"Well, we have to do something!"

"I told you, I'd take care of it." There was no arguing with that note of finality. Linda knew she had to concede, but was hardly comfortable with his plan. Then her husband's face changed as if by another revelation. A new tone of voice accompanied a new topic of discussion. "How did your professor friend know this?"

"He wouldn't say. He said it was very complicated and I would have trouble believing it. He said he was following the Taurus."

"He what?! Why?"

"I don't know. He encouraged me to call the police, but insisted that I leave his name out of it."

"You sure can pick 'em," he said, turning away and moving to the window to look outside.

"I didn't 'pick' anyone," she said, "except you."

"Yeah. Well I'll talk to Marv and his chubby buddy on Monday. I'll deal with the professor later."

"Leave him alone, Mike. If he's involved with them, he must have his own troubles. I'm telling you, I think he was just trying to do the right thing. You leave him alone!"

Michael looked back at her, and Linda glared back.

"I'm going to Williamson's," she said.

"Don't bother. They won't do anything in the open. They were just doing a recon. That's how they'll get to me the next time. Through Liz. The bastards!"

"Mike, what are we going to do?"

"I'll pick Liz up from work tonight. And next week I'll do what Marv suggested. I'll 'communicate.'"

"I don't like this. If Liz is in any danger—"

"Don't worry, Lin. I'll handle it. They're leeches. They'll threaten me, but they still need me to bring home their bacon."

Michael's eyes were focused elsewhere. Although his arm was around her, he was no longer in the room. She knew he was off visualizing a future encounter with Marv and his partner. As suddenly as he left, he returned. "I still don't understand how your professor figures in all this."

"He's not 'my professor,'" she answered. "I want you to leave him alone."

Without any further acknowledgement, Michael headed for the garage. "I gotta get to those lights."

Linda watched him step outside, then retrieved her coat from the closet and followed him outside to hold the ladder.

I should not fear the foe then –
I should not fear the fight!
                              Emily Dickinson, from No. 147

47

It didn't take Michael long to find them. He had seen their car parked outside the Park West Diner before. He parked his truck in the side lot, next to the other delivery trucks whose drivers were having lunch inside.

Walking toward the front door, Michael picked up his own reflection in the fluted chrome shell that encased the eatery. His reflection was distorted, and the surreal appearance matched his temper as he braced himself for what he planned inside.

He had actually been surprised by his own behavior this time. Gone was the instant fury and unrestrained anger that had occurred in the past. This time, he was calculating. He was cool. Forty-eight hours had passed since Liz had been followed. His reaction would be well-planned and easily understood by these two dolts. Yet it would be delivered with restraint—not too little, not too much.

This time was different. This time it was business. Afterwards he still had to work with or around these goons. He would not tolerate another invasion into Liz's space, and that message would be delivered clearly today. But through it all he had to maintain the tricky balance of his lopsided life.

As he entered the diner, through the glass doors he spotted the two men seated at the counter. Marv was sweet-talking a waitress, who was playing along. She had to be doing it for the tip, Michael thought. He could not imagine any woman enjoying the company of that slimy worm. Chubby was enjoying the banter between the two, so neither he nor Marv noticed Michael approach.

Michael had been imagining the attack all weekend, and his dream played out as it had been rehearsed. A roundhouse punch with his right fist knocked Marv off his stool and onto the terrazzo floor with a solid thud. Marv slid for a short distance, coming to rest at the feet of a waitress, who rose on tiptoe as she stopped suddenly to avoid being knocked over.

A woman screamed and the voices of many of the patrons rose in alarm. At a nearby table, a man stood up in protest but made no actual movement to intervene. As if it had been choreographed, Michael swept a box cutter from his left hand to his right, flashing it before Chubby's eyes before bringing it to rest firmly against his throat. This had the desired effect of encouraging Marv's partner to sit still.

"Hey—" yelled a man from behind the counter. He pointed a finger accusingly at Michael.

"You shut up!" Michael yelled, but he was sure the sight of the box cutter did more to silence him than the verbal interdiction. The entire restaurant became instantly silent. Everyone was anxious to see what kind of drama was about to be performed before their front row seats. Michael could actually hear a cell phone being dialed at a nearby booth. Just three digits, probably 9-1-1.

"Am I *communicating* now, Marv?" Michael shouted as the prone figure began to regain his bearings. Rising up on his left elbow, Marv looked up at his attacker. His right hand hovered over his jaw, assessing the damages. "You stay away from my daughter! Do you understand me?"

Marv gave a slight nod.

"Clear?" Michael asked, facing the big man.

A second affirmative nod was forthcoming,

rendered very gingerly in deference to the knife's blade at his neck.

"Okay." With that, Michael rushed out the front door and around to the back, running across the footbridge that led to the large shopping center beyond. Later, from a vantage point there, he saw the police car arrive and leave just a few minutes later. No doubt Marv and his friend would not be inclined to press charges. Later still, Michael took a circuitous route back to Route 46 and returned to his truck. He drove off without anyone in the diner giving him a second look.

Drama's ...
   [Deleted]
   ... Tragedy
                        Emily Dickinson, from No. 741 Lines 1-3

48

"...It will turn cold again tomorrow, highs in the low forties, and rain is likely. So get out there and enjoy the unseasonably warm temperatures and all that sunshine today! Tim?"

"Thank you, Veronica. Metro weather is brought to you by Slomins, who offers you home security you can afford. Call 1-800-Alarm-Me. Get the Slomins Shield."

Paul shut off the radio and closed his eyes, sitting back in the Humvee seat with his face towards the early afternoon sun. This turn in the weather was welcome, and totally unexpected in early December. Added to their good fortune, Paul and Jasper were alone today on the GWB detail, and with no supervisor present, they were taking turns at one hour shifts. Paul now had about forty-five minutes left to catch a nap or maybe read some of that novel he had brought along. It was a typical quiet day on the bridge, and there was no reason to think it wouldn't stay that way.

Paul was growing tired of the Guard, and especially of this guard detail on the George Washington Bridge. There was the boredom, of course. But now with the season fully changed, his perch in the bridge's superstructure was usually a cold place, and the damp air off the river only made it worse. Occasionally Jasper, or one of the other guardsmen, would break things up with a joke or a story. But usually the men were alone, stationed at various locations along the bridge as solitary sentinels.

The walkie-talkie on the seat beside him came alive with Jaspers' voice. "Hey, Swish! Look alive, buddy! We got us one military Humvee westbound, and he's got the hammer down!!"

Paul replaced the helmet on his head, grabbed the radio, and stepped out of his Humvee just as the visitor braked to a stop in the fast lane and then made a sharp left through a narrow passage in the barricade separating the eastbound and westbound lanes of traffic. The vehicle cut perpendicularly across four lanes of traffic, narrowly avoiding several collisions with vehicles accelerating out of the toll lanes. It then pulled up next to Paul's parking spot. Lt. Davis stepped out on the passenger side. Over the shoulder of Davis's driver, Paul could barely make out a civilian, wearing a dark overcoat, seated in the back seat. It looked like the same man who had been with Davis that night at the church in Garfield.

Snapping to attention, Paul turned back to look at Davis, a man who was the focus of attention wherever he went. Paul thought it was the way he carried himself. The man probably slept at "attention."

Without any introduction, Lt. Davis gave an order. "Robinson, you and Wolgamuth saddle up and follow us. We're on our way to a disturbance in Fairlawn."

"Yes, sir!" Paul responded smartly. He brought the walkie-talkie near to his face and relayed the order. "Hey, Jasper! Get your butt down here on the double. We're movin' out!"

Another death-defying crossing of the eastbound lanes by Davis's Humvee brought all traffic to a stop so Paul could follow. Through the cut in the barricade they sped, and then west on Route 80. Jasper plugged the revolving red light into the cigarette lighter and stretched the coiled cord to allow the magnetized base to reach the vehicle's roof. Paul wished Jasper could have done that sooner.

Swinging onto Route 4, they were soon joined by several police cars, their red lights bouncing within their light bars, speeding in the same direction. The police departments of neighboring towns were responding to the request for mutual aid.

Paul pulled his vehicle to the curb on Broadway, right behind Davis's Humvee. Ahead, approaching at a steady pace, was a mob as wide as the broad street and the sidewalks combined. The people were pressed together closer than shoulder to shoulder, and the mass of closely packed humanity was deep, Paul estimated they extended for at least a block. Like a molten lava flow the crowd swept down the street, sliding around parked cars, causing flimsy street signs to vacillate in the stream. In front of them, six police officers—two wearing riot helmets—formed a buckling line that stood no chance of resisting the crowd. The police reinforcements that just arrived rushed to join the line, only to find it was falling back to meet them. Lt. Davis, carrying a bullhorn, led his three men calmly forward. Looking back, Paul saw the man in the black overcoat looking on nervously from the back seat of the Humvee.

As if the volume of a television set was being slowly increased, Paul began to hear the crowd as it approached. Two thousand mouths spoke with one voice—not harsh, but firm, not angry, but determined. "Tyranny, no! Freedom, yes! Tyranny, no! Freedom, yes!"

They didn't walk as much as they flowed, spreading forward as a viscous mass. It was not threatening, nor would it appear to yield to anything short of a stone wall. Certainly the handful of police officers could not challenge it. The officers retreated several yards as the crowd continued to pour forward. Many carried placards, some critical of President

Benson, others making ironic contrasts between the nation's Founding Fathers and today's political climate. One that caught Paul's eye displayed the gold "Don't Tread on Me" Revolutionary-era flag with the coiled rattlesnake. And still the voice of the people filled the street: "Tyranny, no! Freedom, yes! Tyranny, no! Freedom, yes!"

Paul scanned the front line, hoping to re-visualize the mass as an assembly, not a mob. He would pick out one face at a time and study it, imagining for a second that person's occupation, or heritage, or even his faith. One man could easily be a construction worker, the woman next to him, a bank teller. Paul identified a student, a merchant, African-Americans, a truck driver, Asians, perhaps a Presbyterian, a waitress still wearing an apron, maybe a Scandinavian, a Jew, newspaper writer, off-duty cop—

And then Paul spotted him: the large man with the small head. The man from the church who had been hauled off that night for defying Lt. Davis by reciting the First Amendment. As on that night, each word he chanted was spat out, riding a droplet or two of saliva.

The chant of the crowd was suddenly cut by the scratchy sound of Lt. Davis's voice through the bullhorn. "This is Lt. Davis of the New Jersey National Guard. This demonstration is being conducted without the proper permit and is in violation of a Fairlawn ordinances as well as provisions of Executive Order 2177, a Declaration of Martial Law."

As quickly as the crowd had been silenced, it began to buzz. It was an agitated buzz, less than you'd hear near an overturned beehive, but not much less. The buzz increased, however, with Davis's next words. "I am commanding you to disperse, to leave this area immediately. Anyone failing to do so in the next three minutes will be subject to arrest."

Paul had to admire Davis. Even with three automatic rifles, how did Davis expect to hold off this crowd with four soldiers and less than two dozen police officers with side arms?

The crowd began to mill around at its periphery, as if it had lost its direction of just a moment ago. Numerous groups along the front line held conversations on how they should respond to the Lieutenant's edict. Taking advantage of their indecision, the policemen moved forward, forming, temporarily at least, a straighter, more unified line. Paul could sense the tenseness in Jasper's demeanor. Everyone—except Davis—was tense. It was an uneasy feeling for Paul, and he wished he were somewhere else, far away.

A few in the crowd who appeared to be leaders, including the large man with the small head, stepped forward slightly and addressed Davis. "Lieutenant," one of them, who reminded Paul of his young high school Spanish teacher, said, "three minutes isn't very much time to disperse a crowd this size."

"You heard my order," Davis replied through the bullhorn, although the man was less than fifteen feet away. "You've already wasted twenty seconds!"

Paul felt the hairs on his neck rise. A confrontation seemed imminent, even if by default.

The leader took another step forward, perhaps to get away from the grumbling of the crowd which was becoming louder and clearly more frustrated. "All I'm saying—"

Three rapid loud popping sounds erupted from within the crowd. Paul jumped in response even as he tried to understand what they were. Gunshots? Some kind of air bags being popped? Beats on some type of strange drum? Paul didn't know, but as he reacted with surprise, his thumb instinctively released his rifle's safety.

The mini-explosions acted like a signal to the

protestors. The crowd suddenly was rebellious. Voices rose in protest, but not the chanted rally cry of before. Now angry, the voices threw out pointed, insulting remarks directed at Davis and the authorities.

The faces Paul had seen disappeared. It was a faceless crowd now. It was huge. Powerful. Overwhelmingly powerful. Paul suddenly felt afraid. Rationally he had understood their frustration, even their anger. But emotionally, he was more concerned with his own safety, and how the will of this mob was a threat to it.

Paul glanced to his right and spotted a young man in the crowd, a college-aged kid, a student most likely. He was moving forward from the crowd and gesturing wildly with his arms. Paul could not hear the words, but they were clearly venomous, and his lips formed a snarl that distorted his otherwise good looks.

Again, the popping sounds were heard, and Paul felt a rush of adrenaline. He looked frantically about for the source of the noises. He looked to Jasper for reassurance, but his partner appeared confused, too. Out of the corner of his eye he could see the police officers beginning to fall back.

Now the youth jumped into his sight again, and he could hear his words even as he read his lips: "You cocksucker!"

The explosion sounded immense, deafening. So deafening that what followed acted out like a silent motion picture. The college kid's snarl rounded into a frozen position. His eyes bulged with surprise and his face held that expression as it rode his crumpling body down to the street. As if headphones had been reinserted into a jack, the soundtrack returned, and Paul heard the tiny, metallic reverberation of his brass shell bouncing on the street between his boots.

What happened next was accompanied by a

single roar of the crowd. It was an intelligible word with indubitable meaning: "NO!!!!" The crowd surged forward, as if commanded by a single brain. Paul had very little breath in his lungs, for he had gasped and held it upon hearing the popping sounds. Now that breath was forcefully expelled as Jasper's arm jumped under his ribcage and lifted him off the ground. Jasper was running away from the crowd, balancing Paul on his arm. Paul was gasping for air when what seemed only like seconds later, Jasper dropped him into the seat of the Humvee, dove in, and started the engine. A sharp turn to the right, and the vehicle was screaming east on Broadway as a barrage of flying objects struck the roof and windows, sounding like muffled gunfire.

Two ...
> **[Deleted]**
> ... lent –
> Emily Dickinson, from No. 1295 Lines 1-4

49

Linda parted the curtains of the bedroom window and looked outside. Heavy dark clouds had rolled in overnight, shortchanging New Jersey of the already rationed morning light of December. A few brown leaves clung defiantly to some high branches in one of the trees in the yard, cheap seat spectators to the races below as their cousins sprinted along the ground before a brisk wind.

She watched Liz walk down the drive heading for the bus stop. Some traditions die hard, and the Christmas shopping season still brought hope to merchants like Liz's employer despite the austere budgets everyone—except the government—seemed to be adopting these days. So Liz was going in early to prep for the Saturday before Christmas. Liz had tried to be quiet this morning, but Linda's motherly instinct had awakened her before Liz had left her bed. Now that instinct kicked in again as mother felt trepidation concerning her daughter's bus ride to Williamson's.

Despite Michael's assurances that Liz would be left alone and the teen's aura of invincibility that was characteristic of people her age, Linda felt uneasy. But she was reluctant to press the issue. Too many times before her fears had been proven unfounded. Michael was still in business and law enforcement had taken no notice. In fact, black marketeering had become a cottage industry. Several teachers where she worked were supplementing their incomes by selling items from the trunks of their cars. Electronics, apparel, booze, and cigarettes—all were available during lunch and before and after school.

Linda turned to look at her husband, sleeping in today, obviously exhausted. Despite the peaceful image he presented, resting quietly on the pillow balled up in his arms, she knew he was troubled. Restless at night, increasingly argumentative during the day, the pressure he was under was taking its toll. But no more would she urge him to quit. The truck was now theirs, free and clear, and the money that had gone to truck payments was now being deposited weekly in Liz's college account.

Even as Linda realized that Liz was quickly moving toward independence, she was becoming more aware of her need to hold on to Michael. She needed to support him just as she knew he would be there to support her. And to his credit, he was not having flare-ups of jealousy as frequently as in the past. Linda closed her eyes as if to shut out the remembrance. She *had* forgiven him. She had meant it. She was wrong to allow that memory of a half-dozen years ago to surface. It was behind them, and she would leave it there. Quietly, she slipped back into bed, welcomed by the warmth trapped beneath the quilt.

* * * *

She was awakened by the vibration of her cell phone on the nightstand. Picking it up, she did not recognize the displayed phone number.

"Hello?" she said, forcing herself awake.

The voice on the phone was agitated and rapid. It didn't help that Linda wasn't fully conscious. "Mrs. Norton? Uh, this is Chris. Chris Martin."

"Chris? Why—what do you want?" Chris was the last person she expected to call, and only caused her more befuddlement as she struggled to awake. "How did you get this number?"

"Please, Mrs. Norton, don't hang up! I'm sorry, uh, but something's happened."

Michael was now awake, and was struggling to make the transition to waking while turning over to face Linda.

"Chris, what are you talking about? What's happened?"

"Two men—" Chris began.

"Who is it?" interjected Michael.

"SHHH! Chris, two men what?"

"They took Liz. From the bus stop. They dragged her into their car."

"Oh shit! Michael, they've got Liz!"

"Motherfuckers!" Michael threw off the covers and leaped to his feet. Two strides later one leg was in a pair of jeans left on the chair. Following his lead, Linda had run to the closet to throw on some clothes, still speaking into the phone pinched on her shoulder.

"Chris, you mean the bus stop by the mall?"

"No, by my house. Liz wasn't going to work today. I'm sorry."

Michael appeared at the closet door, dressed except for an unbuttoned shirt. "Give me the phone, I'm going after them."

"No. I'm coming, too. You drive, I'll use the phone. Chris, where are you now?" Linda stuck an arm into a shirt as her feet found a pair of flats on the floor.

"I'm trying to follow them in my car. I'm trying to catch up."

"Which way did they go?"

"They turned onto Elm, headed towards town."

Linda covered the phone and spoke to Michael. "They're on Elm Street, heading toward town."

Michael paused as if he were going to argue, but then grabbed his keys off the dresser and moved to the door. "Come on!"

Less than a minute later they were on the road, Michael behind the wheel, Linda repeating what Chris was telling her. "They turned left onto Outwater, heading toward the river."

"Mrs. Norton, I'm so sorry. We didn't mean for anything like this to happen."

"We'll talk about that later. Can you see their car? What kind of car is it?"

"Yes, I've almost caught up to them. It's a big car, GM, I think. Black—or dark brown."

A few more changes of direction and Michael spoke. "They're headed toward the complex where Rudy is." Michael turned abruptly down a street to the left and began to speed in that direction.

Linda grabbed the dash with her right hand as she continued to hold the phone to her ear with her left. "Where are you now?" she asked.

Michael responded to the intelligence with a slight nod and additional pressure to the accelerator.

Moments later, Michael slammed on the brakes at the entrance to the old industrial complex. Screaming out of the drive was a red Camaro with Chris at the wheel, turning left in front of them and speeding away. Clearly alarmed, both his hands were on the steering wheel. There was no sign of a cell phone.

Close behind, the dark sedan followed, the passenger door completely missing, revealing a fat man driving.

"Good luck, Chris!" Michael muttered as he wheeled his car into the complex.

Around corners and down narrow alleys he had lumbered through daily with his delivery truck, Michael now sped with Linda's Civic. The ancient brick buildings were austere during the week, containing the activities in their interiors and keeping their secrets. On weekends, they were quieter still, and the tall narrow windows seemed like disdainful eyes, closed so as not only to deny admittance, but to reproachfully ignore the rare visitor. The car's tires slipped imperceptibly on the slick surface as they hummed over the cobbled alleyways. Here and there a splash through a puddle would punctuate the harmonic drone. Michael and Linda were silent, straining to hear any sound as their eyes peered down shadowed alleys and scanned into alcoves and under canopies for any sign of Liz.

Rounding the last bend before Rudy's, a bizarre scene greeted them. In the drive, not far from Rudy's door, lay the missing door of the sedan, and atop it, lay a motionless man's body in a dark overcoat. Linda averted her gaze from the grizzly sight only to see another terrifying image.

"Look!" Linda pointed to Liz, running away from them before ducking between two of the old brick buildings. Close behind jogged a bare-headed man in a beige trench coat.

"That's Alberto," Michael snarled. Linda opened her door to give chase.

"Wait!" Michael said, putting the car in motion. The force of acceleration closed Linda's door as Michael swerved to avoid Marv and his car door. A few turns later and they arrived at the end of an alley just in time to see Liz dart down another narrow passage. Alberto was running now, fifty yards behind his prey. Linda and Michael jumped out of the car and dashed down the passageway behind Liz.

Their footsteps echoed off the cobblestones in the confines of the passageway. As much from anxiety as the exertion, Linda's breathing became labored. Bursting into a small courtyard, she stopped both to catch her breath and decide on a direction to proceed. Michael grabbed her hand and tugged her to the left, where ahead she saw Liz at the entrance to another passageway, herself gasping for air.

The family reunited, they took flight when they heard the echoes of Alberto's feet. This passageway was short. But to their dismay, it ended in a tiny graveled yard, bounded by the tall brick buildings on two sides and a twelve foot chain link fence at the end. To add to the gloom, many of the building windows had been sealed with bricks and mortar during an ancient reconfiguration. The others were shuttered with plywood or steel. There was no way out except back down the passage.

Alberto's footsteps echoed in the narrow cleft between the buildings. Their pace slowed. There was no need to rush. The hunt was nearly over. His prey was cornered.

Each Norton moved in separate circles, frantically searching for an escape. They moved toward the fence, like an animal would instinctively do, to put as much, though pitifully little, distance between themselves and the mouth of the passage where Alberto would soon appear.

The three were winded from their exertion, hungrily biting at the chilled air. Each gasp burned as it poured down Linda's throat. The air was raw, even though they were now sheltered from the wind. Linda shivered. In her haste to leave the house, she had put nothing on over her shirt.

Linda glanced at Michael, and saw the desperation in his eyes. She looked behind him and saw fear in Liz's eyes. For the first time in her daughter's life, Linda was unable to offer a reassuring look.

As Alberto entered the area, Linda dropped to her knees. She would beg. She would plead. She would supplicate. She would sacrifice herself. She would do anything to save Liz. Linda looked to her left at Michael who had stepped in front of Liz to shield her. He faced Alberto, the look of hopelessness of a moment before replaced by a look of contempt. Even now, cornered and defenseless, he displayed the arrogance and anger that framed his interactions with a complicated world. Could he, with her help, overcome these circumstances? She crawled slightly to her right to better effect a flank attack, or to decoy the monster away from Liz.

She looked at Alberto to see him smile, the slow, pleasurable smile of victory. From within his coat he drew a pistol, a shiny, polished instrument. Its design was as simple as its purpose. One vector was its handle, a second its aim. Linda's eyes became focused on the end of the round barrel, one of the few curves of an otherwise linear machine.

When he spoke, Linda was surprised Alberto's voice wasn't more caustic. His voice had a mellow tone, an ingratiating quality that would have been disarming had he not been armed. "Michael, Michael. We spoke of this before. I told you that a breach of contract would be costly. I warned you! But you stole from me. Now you pay."

Linda shot a fleeting glance at Michael, but her eyes seemed attached to the gun, and to it they returned.

"Alberto, I don't know what you think happened. But we can work it out."

"Do you think I'm stupid?" Alberto's voice was no longer mellow.

Michael raised his hands in a calming gesture to suggest Alberto put the weapon down. "No, I don't think you're stupid. But this—this is stupid. Put the gun down and let's talk like men.

"Talk? There's nothing to talk about."

"Whatever you think I did, I'll repay you…with interest. Just let my wife and daughter go. Put the gun down, before something terrible happens."

Linda saw Michael, steeled for resistance. Somehow he was remaining calm through this. He was able to speak clearly. Linda attempted a swallow, and found that it could not get past her tongue.

Speaking was certainly impossible.

"Michael," Alberto continued, "it's not just the money. It's the trust. Now I know I can't trust you. The only way I can have that trust again is to take something from you—something dear—so that you'll never take such a risk again."

With that, Alberto took a step towards Liz, and Michael moved to shield her.

Alberto sniffed a short laugh. "Whatever. Your daughter…or your wife. I imagine you value them both."

Alberto shifted his weight back in Linda's direction, and she felt her heart jump to her throat. But that was all the motion she could muster. She was frozen to the spot; her back was pressed against the fence.

Alberto sighted down the barrel at Linda. She tried to gasp, but her throat closed. Fear sent a wave of panic throughout her body. After a second Alberto returned his focus to Michael. "Although," he continued, "I think I really want to kill Lizzy. That was your boyfriend, right? Who took out Marv? Marv was a good man. One of my guys who was with me from the beginning. Very loyal. Unlike you, Michael, he did what he was told. I dread to think what will happen when Posha catches Lizzy's little 'hero.'"

With all the strength within her, Linda jumped to her feet, flinging two handfuls of dirt and rocks at the monster as she lunged toward him. Alberto put up his hands to shield against the barrage, then spun around to meet her attack. A quick thrust of his foot caught her jaw with a thud that vibrated through her skull. The force of the blow threw her back against the fence. Pointing the gun at Michael, he froze her husband's advance. Then he leaned toward her with the gun aimed at her head.

"You're dead, bitch!!"

Over ... **[Deleted]**
... plays –
Emily Dickinson, from No. 367 Lines 1-2

50

"How' you holdin' up, Paulie?"

Paul barely looked up at his uncle, seated across the table from the chair into which he dropped. Neither had he hardly noticed the cold, stark meeting room he had just entered, the dark corridors he had just walked, nor the expressionless face of the MP who had escorted him and now stood at attention by the door. The last seventy-two hours had passed in the same way, in a dazed state, with Paul having little awareness of his surroundings and caring even less. But he kept his eyes open as much as he could. Because when he closed them, he saw so vividly, again and again, the image of the young man falling to the ground. He saw the expression on his face, the look of stunned horror that would define the man's final seconds of life.

"I am miserable," Paul said. "And that's as it should be."

"Hey, buck up, Paul. You've gotta be strong through this."

Paul looked at his uncle with detached bemusement. He had always loved Uncle Ken, but now he sounded delusional, totally out of touch and irrelevant in this situation.

"Strong? Cut me a break."

"No! We can fight this. I've got an attorney lined up to come up here and meet with you. Don't give up!"

"An attorney can't change the facts. The fact

is I killed a man. A kid! In front of a thousand witnesses." Paul looked down at his hands folded on the table and then back up at his uncle. He looked him in the eyes, staring, searching, hoping that his father's brother would fully appreciate the sincerity of his next words. "I am so ashamed, Uncle Ken. I have never been so ashamed." Exhausted by the intensity of his feelings, now and over during the last three days, Paul dropped his face into his open hands.

Silence followed. A total void of sound. Only the hum of the fluorescent bulbs overhead could be heard, a steady hum that seemed to Paul to be suggestive of the endless futility: continuing for all eternity.

"What happened, Paul? How did it happen?"

Paul shook his head in bewilderment. "I've been playing it over and over in my head, but I still don't understand it any better than just after it happened." He rubbed his eyes as if then he might better see and understand.

"We were only five or six yards from the crowd. It was Jasper, me, Lieutenant Davis, and one of his men, and just a handful of cops. The Lieutenant had just ordered the crowd to disperse, and their leaders were trying to decide what to do. People on the front line were sort of milling around—not dispersing—but they weren't advancing either.

"Then the leaders and the Lieutenant had words, and everyone got agitated. The crowd started to surge. It was like one giant, living beast. It didn't move so much as it *swelled*. We all had to take a step or two back." Paul looked at his uncle and could see he was listening intently. He, the man who had captivated Paul so often in his youth with his tales, now sat spellbound as Paul told his story.

"Then some people began to get nasty. Saying things. Trying to provoke us.. Us! The ones with the guns! Then there was this noise—like a popping sound. Lots of 'em. It didn't sound like guns, exactly.

But it was still threatening. The fact that we didn't know what the sound was made it sound scarier, I guess.

"And then, suddenly, it was like I didn't want to be there anymore. I was tired of it. All of it. The Guard, the bridge duty, the riots, the protests. I was sick of all of it. Sick of the news reports, the politicians, the crime, the war, the terror attacks, the shortages—" Paul looked down at his hands. They were clenched in fists; held so tightly that they trembled against the table. He felt horror rush from his torso to his mouth, bringing along some stomach acid and maybe even some bile, as well. He swallowed quickly to force the noxious liquid back down.

Paul looked at Ken to be sure he understood. Raising his clenched fists so his uncle could better see, he said, "It was just like this! I got so tense. Like a big spring ready to snap. And then I heard another one of those popping noises, and I flinched, and I pulled the trigger.

"I saw him, Uncle Ken. I looked right at him, and he was looking at me, too. Everything went into slow motion. First he looked shocked, like he was stunned that he actually had been shot. Then he looked confused, just for a second, like 'why does this hurt so much?' Then he grabbed his guts—they were starting to fall out of him—and he sort of drifted to the ground. All the time he had a kind of accusing look in his eyes, a damning look, condemning me forever for what I had done."

Again the silence, again the endless humming.

"So it sounds like an accident to me," Ken said. "You didn't mean to kill the guy. It's certainly not pre-meditated murder. That's why you need the attorney. I gotta be honest with you, Paulie. The media's not showing any sympathy for you. You've gotta get this trial moved to another jurisdiction."

"Why would they show sympathy for *me*? I

killed a man!"

"It was an accident!"

"No!" Paul shouted. Paul saw the MP flinch in reaction to his outburst, but he made no move toward his prisoner.

Not silence this time, but rather his exclamation bounced around the concrete block walls of the room several times.

"No," Paul went on. "It wasn't an accident. It was as clear a case of cause and effect as has ever been.

"Why was I there? To control the crowd. Why was the crowd there? To protest our government and the shit they've been pulling over the years. One scandal after another. One cover-up on top of another. Taxes, debt, more taxes, more debt. Price controls, prices out of control, shortages, black markets. You know that old Wal-Mart store in Lodi? A bunch of guys rented it out, and there's a freakin' black market flea market there almost everyday. Where Wal-Mart couldn't make money, these jokers are! The cops look the other way. Hell, I was in there one day and I saw two guys in uniform shopping—with a shopping cart! And this with the stupid martial law in effect"

"Paulie, Paulie, they started with martial law after the assassination."

"Speaking of which—" Paul glanced up at the MP, realizing that his voice was becoming louder the more he spoke. "Speaking of which," he said in a more subdued tone, "what's become of that investigation? It's been five months since the shooting, and no one's been arrested. You don't even hear about the case on TV. And don't you think it's convenient that just as Benson starts to slide in the polls, Landers gets blown away? And hey, let's declare martial law and blow off the November election, too!"

"You can't be saying Benson had something to do with Landers' death?"

"I'm saying it was convenient. Damn convenient. Anytime some group tries to get some political traction, in steps the National Guard—namely me—to shut them down, to hell with the First Amendment! Sam Adams had an easier time of it under the British!"

"What's this got to do with your case?"

"Like I said, 'cause and effect.' You set something like this in motion, and someone—a lot of people—are going to get hurt. I killed that kid. I'm so beyond sorry. I don't think I can live with the fact that I did it. But if I hadn't been there—if I had been in that crowd, as I should have been, 'cause I get sick at heart every time I do the dirty work of one of Benson's operatives—if I hadn't been there, there would have been some other dumb schmuck who would have pulled the trigger. That's what Benson and those that came before him set in motion."

Paul sat back in the chair and dropped his chin to his chest and again covered his eyes with his hand. Without looking up he added, "Ever notice how the people who are so quick to insist that government take responsibility for everyone's food, clothing, shelter, healthcare, and protection from every imaginable foul deed—ever notice how they never take responsibility when their decisions stomp on the freedoms and crush out the lives of the people they claim to care so much about?"

I ... **[Deleted]**
... called –
Emily Dickinson, from No. 46 Lines 1-2

51

So this was death. Linda was underwhelmed. She had always expected something more. Something more glorious. Maybe a bright light, the sound of trumpets. She didn't know, she just knew this wasn't it.

She had seen Alberto start to squeeze the trigger before she closed her eyes. She opened her mouth to scream, but she could make no sound. Then came the loud explosion. The sound of the gun firing echoed off the brick buildings that surrounded them and now rang like a huge doorbell stuck on one long, loud tone.

She was surprised by the warmth, the comforting warm dampness that engulfed her. The sensation was almost like a steaming towel covering her face.

There was a taste, too. "Taste" was almost too strong a word, for there was little flavor, certainly like nothing she had ever tasted before. But it filled her mouth, and her tongue set out to take its measure. *Definitely not a solid, but hardly a liquid, either. And what's this— ?* Another sensation surprised her as her teeth came together. *–crunchy?*

The crashing sound startled her, and Linda opened her eyes, just in time to see Alberto's body bounce once and come to rest in front of her. His head, or what was left of it, had landed just inches away from her knees. With revulsion, she looked away from the gory scene. Each surprise was greater than the last. Standing in front of her stood Professor Grayson. Both his arms were stretched out in front of him, holding a gun. His eyes were large, focused on the dead man between them. The expression on his ashen face was resolute, as if it had been chiseled from limestone. The arms supporting the firearm were dropping slowly, mechanically.

Linda tried desperately to understand why the professor would be there, armed with a gun. Before she could make sense of that scene, a gasp to her left caused her to face that way. Liz stared back, her hands covering her mouth, a look of horror on her face. Lurching and stumbling, Michael was moving toward Linda, a look of shock etched on his face.

Linda tried to speak, but she again became aware of the crunchiness in her mouth. She expelled what was filling her mouth onto the ground in front of her, right next to Alberto's head. Much of the swill-like fluid was red—blood red—and this color alerted her to draw the clear conclusion. Some of Alberto's brains had flown into her open mouth, and with it, tiny crunchy pieces of his skull. That realization had an immediate effect on Linda's stomach, and soon its contents joined Alberto's regurgitated brains and the blood pooling around his head.

Immediately Michael was there, using his shirt tail to wipe the blood from her face. Then Liz was with her, hugging her., and Linda hugged her back. She felt another wave of nausea, and sensed Michael holding back her hair as she vomited again. All the time, he was wiping her face with his shirt tail and comforting her by holding the damp cloth on her forehead.

When she was through, she drew Michael to her as well, squeezing him close, rejoicing in having both of them, alive, with her, close to her. She glanced down and saw Michael's shirt, now stained with Alberto's blood—a dark red, sticky, mess. She looked away, only to see her own shirt, drenched in places, spattered in others. Then she got a whiff of it all. The subtle metallic smell of the blood, the warm peppery smell of the gunpowder. The hugs of her family were pressing the soaked cloth against her skin, immersing her in the disgusting fluids, so she tried to pull away. She wanted to be out of her clothes—to rip them off and throw them and their blood upon the motionless body before her. But Liz's grasp became stronger, and looking at her face, Linda saw tears streaming down the girl's cheeks. She felt Michael trembling as he embraced them both.

The three of them were one, united in one interlocked embrace. It was a perfect embrace, encircling and containing all of their love. It was a horrible embrace, stained and soiled by the blood of a monster, set in the context of his gory demise. As she continued to embrace them, she looked once more to see the professor, almost motionless, still standing above Alberto's body.

Conviction – ... **[Deleted]**
... Side –
Emily Dickinson, from No. 789 Lines 7-8

52

Russell turned the key in the lock and slowly opened the door. Rufus bounded forward, circling around his master, tail wagging so violently it threatened to throw his pelvis out of alignment. Russell was unable to suppress a slight smile. Otherwise he did nothing more than give the dog a pat before entering the house. He left the storm door ajar to allow Rufus entry when he was ready.

Going straight to his office, Russell ejected the clip from his pistol, then ejected the chambered round and slid it into the magazine. He studied the pieces of the weapon in his hand. With practice, he had become more comfortable loading and unloading it. But now his hands trembled as he held the disassembled gun. It was as alien to him as it was that first day he bought it. He closed his eyes, and the horror of the morning replayed in his mind. He visualized what the gun had done. No, what *he* had done with the gun. Opening his eyes, he placed gun, magazine, and holster in the drawer and pushed it shut. Out of sight, but hardly out of mind.

He returned to the foyer, just as Rufus re-entered, his tail still wagging, though less exuberantly. The man slid a chair from the living room into the foyer and turned it to face the glass storm door and the gloom of the cloudy afternoon. After closing the door, he took his seat. Rufus rested his chin on Russell's thigh, content to share whatever vigil had begun.

Russell absentmindedly petted the dog as he relived the day. As he had done before, he had followed Alberto's men from Paterson. Once again he had been alarmed to see them turn onto the Norton's side street. This time, however, he had been careful not to follow, instead taking up his watch from a secluded spot along the main thoroughfare.

Just as before, he saw Liz board the bus and, predictably, the black sedan begin to follow the bus. He was not ready for what happened next. About half way to the mall where Liz worked, she exited the bus. Russell was about four cars behind the bus when he saw Liz walking along the road toward him. Two cars ahead was the black Ford. It stopped suddenly, and in a perfectly choreographed abduction, the thin man had jumped out of the car, grabbed the surprised girl, and forced her into the back seat. She had had no time to resist. Apparently the driver of the car between Russell and Alberto's men had not taken notice. Everyone was so occupied with their own problems these days. Even an abduction in broad daylight went unnoticed, as the would-be witness soon turned onto a side street.

Russell had continued to follow the sedan at a prudent distance back to Paterson. When it turned sharply to enter an industrial complex through a gate in an ancient brick wall, Russell continued to drive on past. A few seconds later he made a risky U-turn, nearly colliding with an oncoming vehicle. He was signaling for a left turn into the complex when a cherry red muscle car approached and made a right turn into the complex in front of him. The sporty car accelerated to the left around the first building, and Russell, as if he was being sucked into the red car's draft, sped up too. Coming around the corner he saw the red car bear down at full speed on the stopped sedan.

The thin man was outside the car, talking to the driver through the open front passenger door. He glanced up for a second before the car hit him, smashing him and the open car door with a thunderous crunch. The car continued on, dragging them both about ten yards forward in a cloud of dust and debris.

    Thinking fast, Russell ducked his car into an alley and ran back on foot. Peeking around a building's corner, he took in the entire scene. The red car had reversed course, and with spinning wheels and burning rubber, had spun around to exit the way he had come. Liz had seized the opportunity to exit the backseat out the driver's side, and was running deeper into the maze of old brick buildings. Alberto was there, shouting at the heavy driver to pursue the muscle car. The thin man lay motionless on top of the detached car door.

    Russell spun round and put his back to the wall as first the red car, then the black Ford, sped past him towards the gate. Peering around the corner once again, he saw Alberto begin to jog after Liz. Russell started to move in that direction when squealing tires and a racing engine could be heard approaching from the direction of the gate.

    Ducking back into the alley, he saw Linda Norton and her husband arrive in their silver Civic. They paused momentarily at the scene of the carnage, then drove out of sight behind some distant buildings.

    Russell dashed after Alberto, unable to close in on much of the head start he had. Russell had to be careful not to let Alberto know he was behind him. He cautiously looked around each building corner he came to, often just in time to see Alberto disappear around a corner ahead. When Russell jogged past the Norton's abandoned car, both front doors left open wide, Russell had felt a surge of adrenaline. He increased the pace of his pursuit. He wasn't used to this kind of exercise. His legs ached. His lungs screamed for air.

    Coming up to one building, Russell was

uncertain which alleyway to follow. He had taken two steps down the alley to the right when he had heard voices to the left. Drawing his pistol, he moved cautiously down the narrow alley toward the voices.

Just as he approached the corner of the building he heard the voice that had to belong to Alberto.

"You're dead, bitch!!"

Russell swung around the corner in a combative stance. His knees were bent, his two outstretched arms braced the Glock securely. With both eyes open, his focus was on his weapon's front sight. The rear sight was aligned behind it, its two separated halves level with the front sight midway between. Fuzzily out of focus was the body of Alberto, in a stance almost identical to Russell's. The hazy form of Alberto's head sat atop the Glock's leveled sights, just like the bull's-eye target at the practice range.

Russell squeezed the trigger.

The sound was deafening. Echoes off the surrounding buildings served to exaggerate its volume. Worse, Alberto's head immediately exploded as if it were a watermelon, its contents sprayed and splattered across a wide arc before him. Much of his blood and brains seemed to have landed on Linda Norton's face and head.

The queasy feeling hadn't arrived immediately. The deafening boom and the bursting of Alberto's cranium had been rapid and surprising, leaving no time for sensation or reaction. Then the man fell forward and the blood flooded out of his head to blacken the dirt and gravel where he had landed. Only then did Russell realize that he had snuffed out a life.

Yes, he had acted in defense of Linda's life. Yes, Alberto had probably murdered Meredith. Yes, Russell had witnessed that Alberto was ruthless and brutal. But still Russell felt sick. Sick at heart for having taken such a violent and irreversible action. Sick to his stomach for the gruesome way his actions had played out.

He needed a few minutes of deep breathing to calm himself. A few minutes with his eyes closed or else focused on the gray clouds that closed in on the scene from above. A few moments of uncomforting prayer in which he had asked forgiveness for his act.

And then it began. The attempt to apply reason to this most surrealistic of situations. The attempt to convince others of the proper and correct course of action after all propriety had been chucked away.

They should call the police, he had suggested. Explain all that had happened, everything they had seen and had known. He would throw himself on the mercy of the courts, hoping they would find his summary execution of this man, while perhaps not righteous, at least justifiable, maybe even forgivable.

Michael rejected this idea vehemently. Soon after the shooting he had come to Russell, grasped him by the shoulders, and thanked him for saving his wife's life, and most likely that of his daughter and himself as well. But the mention of law enforcement had changed his attitude completely. That, he had said, was not an option.

"But we just can't leave him here," Russell had argued. "Run away like common criminals. We would prove to be no better than he was."

"We gotta get the hell out of here. We gotta leave now, and never look back. This could get very ugly—for all of us. It could drag on for months. And there's no guarantee you'd be cleared, either. Alberto had connections—powerful connections—high up in the government. Who knows how this thing'll play out? No, we gotta get out of here—now."

Russell had been surprised how weak he had been. He had turned to Linda for support. She seemed willing at first to agree, but a quick glare from

Michael and she quietly had shaken her head, indicating she could not agree with Russell.

Then Liz had begun to cry. "What about Chris?" she had asked.

"Later," Michael had retorted. "We gotta get out of here—right now!"

Grimly they had all hustled back to the Norton's car. Michael drove them back through the narrow alleys and shadowy lanes of the complex, past the motionless body of Alberto's goon, to the alley where Russell's car was parked.

On the way, Russell had asked about the red Camaro. Michael had explained that the driver was Liz's boyfriend. "I'll take care of him," he had said. Then, speaking to Liz in the backseat, "Liz, see if you can get him on the phone."

"I'm on the phone with him, now," Liz had answered.

Russell followed the Nortons out of the complex. Then the Norton family turned left towards Garfield, Russell turned right toward Parsippany.

Now he sat and awaited the inevitable. At any moment a police cruiser would pull up in front of the house. No—an unmarked detective's car. Yes, this would be a job for detectives. They would come up to the door and confront him. Russell would be unable to deny anything. They would arrest him quietly. No one in the neighborhood would even notice. He would tell them where they could find the weapon. He would explain it was self-defense—he wouldn't mention Linda, or any of the Nortons, for that matter. By agreeing to leave the scene as he had, he seemed to have made a pact with Linda's family, and he would keep that pact as long as he could. By leaving the scene he would also seem to have implicated himself, thus he would be arrested until this whole thing could get sorted out.

The soft fur between his fingers reminded Russell of Rufus. Yes, he would have to ask the detectives to make arrangements for the dog. Russell felt as helpless as he knew the dog would feel in a few hours when Rufus, too, would be taken away.

Hour followed hour. Russell's mind continued to race. Surely the police would have had a crime scene investigation unit on the scene by now, and they must be finding, marking as evidence, and analyzing the details that would eventually lead them to him. What had he left at the scene? Footprints perhaps. Tire tracks from his car—although they were far from both deaths. A shell casing. Yes, he had left the brass on the ground. He must have touched it when he had loaded the Glock's clip. Maybe only a partial print on the rim of a shell casing. No, with his luck, he had left a thumb and forefinger print big as day on the smooth brass casing.

Then there's the paraffin test. The police would be able to prove that he had fired a gun recently by the powder residue thrust into tiny crevices of the skin on his hands. He could wash his hands real thoroughly—maybe that would be enough. But why bother? By fleeing he had already acted as a criminal. Why should he try to cover it up any further? It was self-defense. Justifiable homicide. Manslaughter at the very worst. It wasn't like it was pre-meditated.

Or was it? He had been stalking Alberto for weeks. Alberto was a hoodlum. What if the authorities were watching him too? What if they had noticed Russell stalking—even following—Alberto? A sense of panic gripped Russell. How many surveillance cameras had he driven past during his "undercover investigation?" How many traffic cameras, security cameras at nearby businesses? Maybe even cameras on the buses that Liz had ridden? Was that what was taking so long? Were the police reviewing hours and hours of surveillance footage?

It was dark when Rufus emitted a little

whimper and Russell realized he must be hungry. He got up from the chair and moved to the kitchen, turning on a light. He added some dry dog food and water to Rufus's bowls and presented them to the appreciative animal. *Now is when they'll come*, he thought. *The police will come now as I resume even this most trivial of my daily routines.*

The ringing phone startled him. *Yes, that's it. They'll call me on the phone.* "Mr. Grayson, could you come down to police headquarters? We need your help to clear a few things up." *Yes, that's how they'll do it.*

Russell took a deep breath, and expelled little of it as he answered the phone.

"Russ, it's me, Winnie McDonald. I just heard on the news."

Russell's confusion was complete. Why would his friend, the business professor, be calling him? "News? What do you mean?"

"Oh, I had assumed you knew. I'm sorry. It's the lead story on tv—CNN's playing the same video clip over and over. The men they think killed Meredith are dead."

"What?"

"I doubt it's consoling news; still, I hope it does bring you some sense of closure."

Russell was speechless. Caught totally off-guard, he was as stunned as if he had been hit by a taser.

"Russ, are you okay?"

"Oh, I'm sorry, Win. This news—it's just so shocking, so unexpected—I'm sorry,"

"No need to apologize. We can only begin to guess what it's been like for you since—" Winnifred paused for an awkward moment. "—since then. I'm just glad the bastards got what was coming to them."

"Thanks Winnie. For the call… for caring. For all of your support since it happened."

* * * *

Russell flipped on the television using the remote, and stood dumbfounded. He couldn't sit down or move from the spot. His attention was glued to the image on the screen: a distant view of the area where Liz's boyfriend had struck and killed one of Alberto's men with his car. A yellow tarp was in the center of the scene, doubtlessly covering the goon's body.

"...grisly scene. In all, three men are dead. Two were found at this industrial complex in southeastern Paterson. The identity of one man has not been released, pending notification of next of kin. He was apparently run down by an automobile. Authorities say evidence at the scene suggests the vehicle that struck and killed this man was dark blue in color. Initially, it was reported that the car was believed to be red. Later this afternoon, that information was updated to indicate the victim was struck by a dark blue car.

"The second man found here was identified as Alberto Gonzalez, who allegedly has ties with organized crime. Police speculate that he was killed by a rival crime organization in a turf war. He was killed by one bullet to the head in typical mob rub-out fashion.

"A third man, Pasqual Eschevera was killed in a firefight with police in Elmwood Park. He is alleged to be a member of the same crime syndicate run by Gonzalez. Police said a short chase began after police attempted to stop the man for a motor vehicle violation. Allegedly, he stopped his vehicle on Molnar Drive and began shooting at police. The police returned fire and struck Eschevera. He was pronounced dead at the scene. John Weaver, CNN News, reporting."

"Thank you, John. We now take you to Washington, D.C., where Special Agent Phillip Burns is speaking live at a press conference at Secret Service Headquarters:"

"...cooperation with the Paterson Police, the New Jersey State Police, the F.B.I., and an investigative unit of the Army National Guard, have been investigating what appears to be a gang-land slaying of three members of a local organized crime organization. One of the deceased, Alberto Gonzalez, has been identified as a prime suspect in the assassination last July of Presidential candidate John Landers and four of his aides in Fort Wayne, Indiana. We have irrefutable evidence that Mr. Gonzalez and two others flew from New Jersey to airports near to Fort Wayne shortly before the murders, and flew back to Newark shortly afterward. We are currently corroborating additional evidence that strongly suggests that these three individuals were involved with the shooting of Mr. Landers. We will now take a few questions, but we remind you that this investigation is still under way and that we may not be able to comment in some cases. Yes?"

"Can you speak as to the motive Gonzalez and his accomplices may have had for committing the assassination?"

"I'm sorry, we cannot comment at this time as that is still under investigation."

"Can you give us the names of the accomplices?"

"Those names are not being released until notifications have been made to next of kin. As soon as those notifications are made, we will release the names to the press.

"Will the results of this investigation lead to the lifting of martial law that was imposed immediately after Mr. Landers' assassination?"

"That will be the President's call. I'd rather not speculate at this time. Thank you ladies and gentlemen."

"That was Secret Service Special Agent

Phillip Burns reporting that three men who died today in an apparent gang-land slaying have been identified as prime suspects...."

Russell watched five cycles of the news broadcast before switching the television off and returning the chair to the living room.

How ...
[Deleted]
... concern –
Emily Dickinson, from No. 1150 Lines 1=4

53

Only a small desk lamp burned in the spacious office just off the hallway that led to the Oval Office. With the sun set, no light snuck past the drawn blinds. The spacious couch and comfortable armchairs were barely discernable in the shadows. The light from the lamp fell on a small circle in the center of the desk and bounced onto the face and dark framed eyeglasses of the man at work there.

It was four-thirty in the afternoon, and Larry Drollinger was sitting at his desk for only the second time today. He did so mostly out of exhaustion. He had long ago given up on the fantasy of believing that being Chief of Staff to the President of the United States was a prestigious but cushy job. If Benson was appearing to age rapidly during his term in office, then his Chief of Staff must resemble Rip Van Winkle.

Dialing Smothers, one of his aides, he alerted him that the President would be traveling tomorrow: a spur-of-the-moment decision to go to a fund raiser in Chicago he had declined a month earlier.

"Yeah, I know it's short notice. But the President believes he can shore up his position with the business community with an address to industry leaders there. The fund raiser is icing on the cake."

Larry covered his eyes as Smothers vented. He gave him thirty seconds then uncovered his eyes. The glare from the desk lamp seemed especially harsh.

"Absolutely you need full Secret Service workup. The climate being what it is, we can't take any chances. Yeah. Yeah. I don't care. Make it happen!" Larry dropped the receiver onto its cradle. He didn't have time for Smothers' excuses.

He didn't have time for a lot of things. He still had to go over that speech in front of him on the desk, to check it for any places Benson might screw it up. Larry felt like he spent half the day looking for snares and the second half clearing up Benson's gaffes. The man couldn't remember his lines from one day to the next. And if he *ad libbed*, well, then the few members of the hostile press would have a field day. Benson prided himself on being able to speak "off the cuff." "That's why the people like me," he'd say, "'cuz I speak from the heart, not off a teleprompter." *That's what's going to get you impeached*, Larry thought, *and God help the rest of us*. Benson had no idea what had been done in his name. He had no idea how much he owed his success to Larry and his people. He also had no idea that so many of the public were against him. Larry's friends had been able to manipulate the polling results, but that couldn't last forever. Some of Benson's friends in the press were beginning to question things they would have accepted without question six months ago.

Larry opened the loose leaf notebook containing the speech and flipped to the first page. Then the phone rang—his private line.

"Drollinger."

"It's done."

Larry looked toward his office door. *No one nearby. It didn't pay to get up and close the door. This call wouldn't last long. They never did.*

"It's tied off?" Larry asked.

"Tied off. Almost as planned."

"It took you long enough, I gotta say."

"The man had to grieve. If we had moved too

quickly, he could have botched the whole thing. Now we're golden."

"Wait, what do you mean 'almost'?"

"There was an unexpected actor. A kid. Came out of nowhere. We'll monitor him. Control him. Liquidate if necessary."

"Another round of killing?" Larry said this in a hushed whisper. *He should have closed the door.*

"We'll do what we need to do. You're covered."

With that the phone line went dead.

But then I promised ne'er to tell –
How could I break My Word?
                              Emily Dickinson, from No. 416

54

"You're leaving the car in the street?" Linda asked as Michael pulled to the curb.

"Yeah," Michael said. He looked at his wife and smiled with an attempt to reassure. On the drive home, Michael's mind had been racing. Now it slammed to a stop. In this car were the people he loved, all he treasured, all that mattered. How close he had come to losing them today. Linda still clutched his hand. She hadn't let go since they left the industrial complex. She wasn't trembling as much as before. With her free hand she had wiped her face numerous times during the short drive. He hadn't let go either. As much as she appeared to need him, he needed her. So he had driven home with one hand on the steering wheel and one eye on the road, the other darting to the rear view mirror to check on Liz in the back seat. "I need to take care of some things. I've been thinking about this all the way home. We really need to cover our tracks. I'd like both of you to go inside and clean up. Put all the clothes you're wearing in a garbage bag. Towels and washcloths, too. And remember," he said, "we don't mention anything that happened today to *anyone*."

He glanced into the back seat. Liz was talking in hushed whispers on Linda's cell phone. "Chris is coming over here?" he asked.

"Yeah. He'll be here in a few minutes."

He had tried to keep his family separate from the sordid side of his life. He had shared little with

Linda, almost nothing with Liz. But now there was no separation. All the ugliness, the vile stench of it, had leaked through and soiled them, leaving a permanent stain they could never remove.

Linda attempted a smile and squeezed his hand more firmly. Only she was able to respect him after he nearly failed her so miserably. He owed both Linda and Liz a better outcome in the next phase of this crisis.

"Go on," he encouraged her. "I'll be in to change in a minute."

The two women walked to the house with their arms around one another. Supporting each other. As they always did. As he always wished he could.

He was going to make some changes. That he had already decided. He would go legit. Even if it meant working for someone else. He'd even take less money. He needed his self-respect. He needed his family's safety.

He would re-evaluate his associations. Rudy was a friend. But was he a good friend? Rudy had lured him into a criminal life that only spiraled more out of control once Alberto got involved.

And there was Chris. The boy had guts. He took action and made a difference. He had made much more of a difference than Liz's own father. Had Liz seen this in Chris? What blinded Michael that he couldn't see it?

Most amazing was the English professor. If he hadn't shown up when he did…and with a gun, no less. How had he shown up? Why had he shown up? These were questions Michael couldn't begin to answer, though his first suspicions were clearly wrong. Twice, now, the professor had been at the right place at the right time. And like he had with Chris, Michael had dismissed the professor and hadn't given him a chance. He hadn't listened to Linda, as he hadn't listened to Liz. All he had heard was the voice of the jealous little loser inside him.

The voice of someone who lacked confidence in himself or sufficient trust in Linda and Liz.

* * * *

Michael was standing just inside the garage as Chris turned the red Camaro into the driveway. "Pull your car in here," he said, stepping aside.

Chris nodded, and inched the car inside. Once in, Michael pulled the door down behind him.

Liz ran into the garage from the kitchen, embracing Chris as he got out of the car. Michael acknowledged the glare of defiance that Liz shot his way as she hugged her boyfriend and continued to hold him.

After a few moments, Michael cleared his throat. "Liz, why don't you go inside for a few minutes while Chris and I talk."

Liz turned to look at Chris, giving him an encouraging smile, and then gave him another hug before peeling away. She was still watching him over her shoulder as she walked back up the steps into the kitchen and closed the door behind her.

"How are you, son?" Michael asked. At first it felt strange using that moniker. But Michael was working on the biggest sale of his life, and this customer had to be won over. After hearing the word, it didn't seem all that strange after all.

"Okay, I guess," the boy answered, staring at his sneakers.

Michael took a few steps forward. "That was a gutsy thing you did today. It took a lot of courage. You probably saved Liz's life."

Chris looked up and turned his head towards the man, looking Michael in the eyes for the first time.

"I—I want to thank you," Michael continued, extending his hand. "To tell you I respect you."

Chris stood a little taller now. He grasped the

hand and said, "Thank you, sir."

Michael clutched the boy's elbow with his left hand and gave two emphatic shakes with his right. The pair continued to look at one another, saying nothing.

At last Michael broke free, and grabbing a lawn chair from against the wall, he opened it and gestured for Chris to sit. He opened the chair's twin and sat in it, the two seats just inches apart.

Still there was silence. Then Michael cleared his throat. "Have you told anyone about what happened today?"

"No, sir."

"Anyone at all?"

"No."

"Not even your parents?"

"No!"

"Okay. Okay." Michael leaned back in the chair. He realized his leg was jittering at a rapid rhythm. He clamped both hands on his knee to attempt to contain it.

"Mr. Norton, I didn't mean to kill that man." Chris's lips began to tremble. "I mean, not at first. I, I saw them grab Liz, and she was kicking, but he pushed her into the car. Then I follow them to that old factory. It looked abandoned. I was scared. Scared they were going to hurt her…to kill her.

"Then he got out of the car, and I thought, 'what can I do?' I thought they might kill her right there. So I gunned it to get there faster, then I thought, I can stop this, so I went even faster, and I…I aimed right for him. …It was terrible."

Michael leaned forward and put a hand on Chris's knee. "It's okay. I don't know what else you could have done. And I'm glad you did what you did. I think you're right. They probably would have killed Liz." Michael shuddered as the realization of what he was saying hit home.

"I killed him!"

"It was self-defense, Chris. Like you said, if you didn't kill him he would have killed Liz. It gave her a chance to get away."

Chris dropped his head into his hands and sat motionless. Michael put his hand on the boy's shoulder. "It's okay," he said.

After a moment, Michael spoke again, "Chris?"

Chris looked up, no longer with an expression of remorse. A cold look, spawned by harsh realities, had taken its place. Already this morning Michael had seen similar changes in Linda and Liz. Whether it was shock or the urgent need to move on, they were all finding ways to cope.

"Chris, I need to ask a favor. I know twenty-four hours ago you probably thought I was a jerk. You may still feel that way. Can't say as I blame you." Michael offered a weak smile, an invitation to reject his suspicion. Chris wasn't accepting.

Michael continued. "But like I said. I respect you now. I have a lot of respect for you." He was running out of bait and the hook was untouched. "What I'm asking, I'm asking for Liz. For my wife, too. And for me. It's really important to our whole family."

"I don't—"

"No, of course you don't. Listen, Chris. I got a few years on you. I got experience you don't have yet. And what I mean is, well, things don't always turn out like they do on the police shows on TV. The guilty guy doesn't always get convicted. But the innocent guy sometimes does! It's not so black and white as you might think." Michael studied the boy's face, but couldn't get a sense of what he was thinking. He went on.

"What I mean is, that man you hit today: he was a bad man. He was scum. He enjoyed hurting people, torturing people. The world's a better place with him gone.

"But that doesn't mean you're in line for a medal. If the police find out you were there, they'll ask questions. Hours of questions. And if they don't like your answers—well, welcome to the criminal justice system.

"And it won't be just you. They'll question Liz, and me, and Liz's mom. This whole thing could get very ugly. I mean, even uglier." Michael paused to take another reading of Chris's face.

"What do you want me to do?" Chris asked at last.

"I want you to keep everything that happened today—everything—a secret. Tell no one. Not your parents. Not your friends. Don't even talk to Liz about it. She doesn't need to re-live none of this again. Can you do that?"

"And if I do?" Chris's eyes glanced furtively at the kitchen door.

"This isn't a deal, son." Michael was surprised how easy the word flowed out of his mouth this time. "The restrictions on you and Liz, they're gone. I told you: you've earned my respect. I'm not trying to win you over by offering you access to Liz. I'm hoping you'll see how much this will *help* Liz. And you. All of us."

Chris looked off into space, as if he were disconnected from this place and somewhere far away. Michael thought he was much more energized when he returned. "Okay, I'll do it."

"No one. You will mention this to no one?"

"Right. Not a soul. You have my word."

This time Chris grasped Michael's hand. They were partners now. Partners in crime.

"Now, about your car," Michael said, rising from the chair and moving to inspect the car's grill.

"What about it?"

"Did you see this? It's smashed pretty good. If the cops see this they're going to ask you about the accident. The accident you never reported."

"Oh, yeah."

"You own this car?"

"Yeah, my parents got it for my birthday."

"But is it registered to you? Pop the hood."

"Uh, no."

"Damn. But you think you own it?" Michael added, studying the Camaro's engine.

"I do own it."

"So if you decided to soup it up, your parents wouldn't have a problem with that, would they?"

"I don't think so."

"Good. 'Cause you and I are going to do a little project together. Sort of a mentoring thing. We're going to turbocharge this puppy. Right here in my garage. Tell your parents I've got the tools and we took it apart enough that it won't run."

"Really?"

"Yeah, come over a couple of nights a week and we'll work on it. And the first thing we're gonna do is we're gonna change out this grill and cowling."

"I can't believe you'd do this."

"I owe you, Chris. I owe you big time." Michael turned back to the car. He didn't like sounding mushy. "Not that this car needs a turbocharger. I saw you haul ass out of that factory complex today. You were really moving! What happened to the fat guy following you?"

"Oh, wow, it was like the strangest thing!" Chris was animated for the first time. "He caught up to me at a traffic light, and there was too much traffic for me to get away. Besides, there was a cop sitting right at the gas station at the corner, so I couldn't run the light or anything.

"So, anyway, the fat dude is right behind me, and I see him open his door to get out. And I'm thinking, maybe I'll run toward the cop car. But then the cop car puts on his red lights—I guess he saw the missing door on the fat dude's car. So the fat dude gets back in his car and peels out of there! The cop puts on his siren and chases after him. And me—the light turns green and I just drive away."

The kitchen door opened and Linda appeared. "Michael, I've been listening to the news on Channel 12. I need to tell you something." A slight head gesture indicated she wanted a private audience.

"It's okay," Michael responded. "You can talk in front of Chris. He's cool." Michael was happy to see Chris smile in response.

"Well," Linda began, "they said *three* men were killed today. Two at the factory and a third man in a shoot-out with police!"

Michael and Chris exchanged surprised glances.

"And get this:" Linda continued, "they said the car that struck the man at the factory was a *dark blue car!*'

"Dark blue?" Michael questioned. "Are you sure."

"Sure I'm sure. They keep saying the same thing over and over. I heard them say it three times, already."

"Why would they think it was blue?" Michael dropped into the lawn chair to try to get his head around this news.

How... **[Deleted]**
... gun
Emily Dickinson, from No. 118 Lines 5-6

55

"Agent Burns, please. Russell Grayson. Thank you." Russell sat back in his desk chair and listened to the recording when his call was put on hold. It was yet another reminder to take action if you see suspicious behavior. 'If you see something, say something," it concluded.

After exchanging pleasantries, Russell began," I saw your press conference on tv."

"Yes, of course. I've been meaning to call you, but so much has been going on. It looks like we got 'em. All three of them. I hope that fact brings you some peace."

"How can you be sure they were the ones?" Russell leaned forward, focused on every word to come.

"Our investigation is tying things together pretty tightly. It was them. I'm certain of it."

"I see," Russell said. "It's just that, I was wondering: why did it take so long to find them? They didn't seem to be highly trained professionals."

"That's how it works sometimes," Burns said. "Sometimes the leads come together easily, other times they have to be rearranged like a huge jigsaw puzzle."

"I get that," Russell persisted. "But they captured Lee Harvey Oswald within hours of Kennedy's assassination. You're telling me that with all the advances in law enforcement, with all the resources of the Secret Service, the F.B.I., and God

236

knows who else, that you couldn't find these guys in four months? And that you only found them because some other mobsters got to them first?"

"I understand you're frustrated, Mr. Grayson. But we did everything we could—legally—to find these individuals and bring them to justice. You're right, though. Now we're looking for some new criminals."

"The Secret Service is looking for them?"

"Sorry. I said 'we,' as in law enforcement. The Service has no jurisdiction in these homicides. Paterson P.D. is investigating, aided by the Organized Crime Unit of the State Attorney General's office. Of course, we'll assist them in any way we can."

"I see," Russell responded. Burns was as polished as ever, a real credit to the Secret Service. Russell wondered which was the more important trait for an agent—a knowledge of law enforcement or the ability to stay cool in times of chaos, to remain professional amidst blatant ineptitude? "Still, there's one thing I just can't come to understand: why would these neighborhood thugs get involved with an assassination?—interstate, no less!"

"I can't comment on that; we're still investigating that, too. When we get the answer, and I'm free to release the information, I'll be in touch. It was good hearing from you again, Mr. Grayson. Unfortunately, I'm in the middle of something and I really need to go. I just hope this helps bring this sad chapter to a close for you."

Russell hung up the phone and sat back in his chair. The call had been a fishing expedition. But he hadn't expected to catch much. The Voice had already been proven correct on so much of his information. Whether Burns' was just inept or complicit had not been determined. Russell didn't expect a phone call like this to resolve that question, and he didn't have the expertise or resources to pursue it further. Besides, the American electorate shared in the culpability. Even if the choices they made were only marginally worse than the alternative, they had repeatedly endorsed less efficiency and more corruption.

Russell figured that Burns would expect him to call. If he didn't pretend to be ignorant, then Burns might conclude that he knew something he shouldn't.

Additionally, Russell hoped to get a sense as to whether or not he was still a suspect. News reports continued to characterize the killing of Gonzalez and his men as a mob hit. They continued to allude to the mysterious dark blue car. That information was extraordinary in its inaccuracy. Even the few fender-benders Russell had experienced were enough to convince him that incompetence could not explain away this blunder. Which meant that it was not a blunder, but a means to throw others off Chris's trail. Or was it a signal to Chris and Russell that the trail was not to be followed? Or was it a trick to make them believe that was the case? That was the problem with conspiracy theories: they were just theories.

Far from closure, these uncertainties tormented Russell. He may have avenged Meredith's murder, but that was not as comforting a condition as he might have imagined. This was compounded when he realized that Gonzalez was just a pawn on a huge chessboard. The chess player was still at large. And if Alberto was a pawn, what would the queen look like?

Beyond what Meredith had meant to him as a lover and a partner, Russell was appreciating more and more her contributions to education and politics. To truly avenge Meredith, the truth that she advocated needed to be vindicated. When she was silenced, there was one less of the very small minority who understood liberty's origins and how it could be preserved. Whether correctly attributed to de Tocqueville or Tytler, the comment regarding the durability of American government was being proven true in every election cycle: "The Republic will cease to exist when the majority discovers it can vote itself largess out of the public treasury." The Democrat Party had caved on this issue long ago. The Republicans had also, though arguably to a lesser degree. What were the chances the Liberty Tree Party could persevere, especially with its leaders being assassinated? One thing Russell had learned over the past few months was that the truth alone was not always sufficient.

As he did so often when he felt frustrated, he turned to Dickinson's poetry. He grabbed the worn copy on his desk, and turned to a page at random.

It ... ***[Deleted]***
         ... Loneliness –
                    Emily Dickinson, No. 405 Lines 1-2

56

There was no place to sit in this part of Newark Liberty Airport. All the seating was ahead, near the gates. So he was standing here with the others, waiting to greet arriving passengers.

The arriving flights monitor had displayed "ARRIVED" for Karen's flight, and a surge of people coming into the main concourse had confirmed it. But Russell bided his time. Since Karen was on crutches, she would be one of the last to get here. There was no doubt she would decline a wheelchair, or any kind of assistance, for that matter.

Indeed, he was the only one left when he saw her, taking large strides with the crutches then swinging her body forward freely. It reminded him of her as a child, always swinging the highest, making the merry-go-round spin the fastest, hanging most precariously from the top of the jungle gym. It was no surprise that she became a pilot of supersonic fighter jets.

She caught sight of him and smiled. It was that electrifying smile she flashed everywhere. The smile that revealed so many teeth, made straight by those many months in braces. The smile that wrinkled her nose just a tiny bit. The smile that enlarged her eyes while bringing extra life to them at the same time. Just like the smile that Meredith had smiled when she was happy, which had been often.

He stepped forward to embrace her, only to wait as she juggled one crutch to another hand to free one of her arms to reciprocate. His arms got mostly knapsack, a huge bag strapped to her shoulders. His kiss of "welcome home" was much better than the kiss of "good-bye" he had pressed on her cheek shortly after the funeral.

"Gosh, Dad, you've lost so much weight!" She was still smiling, but the look of concern was dimming it. He had seen that look before, too, also on Meredith's face.

"Yeah, well, sometimes I'm just not hungry." *Snap out of it! This is supposed to be a happy homecoming!* "You look great, though, if you ignore the plaster cast. How was the flight?"

"Fine. They fly so slow, though! I had a window seat and the whole way I kept thinking, 'turn on the afterburners, already!' They offered me a wheelchair, but I said 'no.' I couldn't wait to see you."

The glow had returned, but it was quickly dimmed as she again turned serious. "How are you doing, Dad? Really?"

"I'm—I'm coping. Yeah, I'm doing okay."

She reignited the smile, perhaps more of a reassurance for him than a response to his answer.

"Can I take your bag?"

"No, it's fine. Not too heavy. It's much lighter than the pack I carried twenty miles in 'Basic.' I kept telling them, 'I'm a pilot, not an infantryman! I have checked luggage!'"

He smiled at her joke as he turned to walk with her towards the exit. "I expected you to be in uniform."

"Nope. Strictly 'civvies.' Guess they thought the military wouldn't look too strong on crutches. No, it's strictly R&R until this bone heals. I reckon they figure 'what the hell, send her home, at least she won't be eating on Uncle Sam's dime.'"

"'Reckon?'"

"Damn! I keep using that word! There's this

guy in our unit from Arkansas. He 'reckons' before he does anything. Next thing you know, everybody in the battalion is saying it."

"Well then, I reckon I should say 'Welcome home, Lieutenant Grayson.'"

* * * *

They had stopped at the Longhorn Restaurant for dinner. "There's not much to eat at home, anyway," he had said. The dim light in their booth fell softly on Karen's face, modeling its feminine curves. Her femininity was enhanced set against the masculine decorations of the restaurant, the paintings of cowboys in their saddles, the bull's horns and branding irons on the walls. She was as beautiful as her mother, and as strong-willed and gutsy, too.

Half of her steak was gone when she pointed at his plate with her fork. "Seriously Dad? You've hardly touched your dinner."

"Yeah, well, I guess it's all the excitement. Knowing that you'll be home for a while. Rufus is going to go nuts! I think he already senses something's up, by the way I've been acting. Wait until he sees you!"

She sawed off another bite before asking, "So what do you do with your time now?"

"Oh, you know. The usual things. Chores around the house, take care of the dog, grade some papers—things like that."

"Dad— you are, you know, moving on, right? It's what Mom would have wanted. You know that, right?"

"I'm doing what I can. Teaching, the job, that helps me think about other things. I think I'm going to be okay."

His daughter studied him for a moment, then returned to her steak. "Well, I'm going to be watching you. And if I see that you're down in the dumps, I'm going to take action."

"I'm sure you will. It's good to have you home, Karen."

* * * *

She finally broached the subject hours later, reclining on the couch, a laptop open next to her, Rufus asleep on the floor beside her. "I've been reading everything I can find about the men—the men killed in Paterson last weekend. I just can't figure out what motivated them to do what they did."

"We'll probably never know, Karen. The world is full of crazy people."

"That's not enough for me. Are you telling me it's enough for you?"

"It's like I said before. I'm learning to cope."

* * * *

Karen had gone to bed. Russell was still restless. He felt uneasy not sharing everything with Karen. But he knew it was for the best. It was enough that he carried the burden, unloading any of it on her would be unfair.

Besides, he had trouble understanding himself why he had bought the gun in the first place. Had he subconsciously recognized some tipping of the scales? Had he somehow sensed the addition of a camel's back breaking straw that had irretrievably altered the balance and dumped a civil society over to reveal a jungle ruled by brute force? He was reluctant to admit that his intellectual powers had been overruled by animalistic instincts. Yet that was the reasonable conclusion. His lack of understanding contributed to his fears.

He didn't know why so many commercial relationships had been compromised by government leaders in Washington who lacked faith in the people to make basic economic decisions. Meredith would have tried to explain it to him. She, who had predicted so much, and so many of whose predictions had come to pass. But even she could not have predicted her own murder. She, who had understood so much, had not completely understood that greed and lust for power could overcome the most basic tenets of a society. He did fully appreciate why so many of the people held these leaders in low esteem.

He had trouble understanding much of the world and his new place in it. He couldn't grasp the bond that now linked him in such an unusual way to a family he barely knew. He found himself often thinking of Linda. He would chastise himself—she was married, after all. Then he would consider her again, as someone more than a stranger, if perhaps, not justified to expect his devoted protection.

Had that truly been his motivation, to protect an innocent woman and her family from a criminal attack? Or was it merely a convenient cover for his own pre-meditated behavior as an assassin? He had stalked Gonzalez for weeks. He had offered him no chance to surrender. He had shot him from behind. Russell trembled as he dared equate his quest for revenge with the tyrant's quest for control. Surely he was better than that. He *had* to be better than that.

He went to his study and took a book off the shelf. It was an early edition of Emily Dickinson's poetry. The original owner had penned numerous notes and comments in the margins. Maybe his insights might help Russell to better understand Miss Dickinson. Maybe the poetry might help him better understand himself. "Talk to me, Emily," he whispered. He sat at his desk and began to read. The Glock lay in the drawer just inches away.

THE END

Acknowledgements

Once again the author is indebted to his friends in the Montville Writers' Group whose critiques and encouragement helped complete this novel. By name, they are Gill Otto, J. D. Rule, Christine Balne, Tina Book, David Reuter, and Betty Bowers.

Emily Dickinson's poetry was excerpted from *The Complete Poems of Emily Dickinson*, edited by Thomas H. Johnson and published by Little, Brown & Company. That the publisher allowed this use is gratefully acknowledged. We wish Harvard University Press, which holds the copyrights to Miss Dickinson's poetry, had been similarly inclined.

Rebecca Curcio has received credit for creating my portraits for all my book covers, including this one. All other photography on the cover is the work of the author.

The author also recognizes the patience and support of his wife during the creative process.

Rich Polk

About the author

Rich Polk has enjoyed diverse careers in law enforcement, risk management, accounting, teaching, and consulting. Now semi-retired, he hopes to devote more scheduled time to his writing. Readers have enjoyed his first novel, *The Boarder on Monroe Street*, and his *Patchwork, a collection of short stories*. He recently relocated to Monroe, New Jersey (purely coincidental to the novel's title) where he lives with his wife, Michelle, and pursues his interests in photography, travel, railroads, and ornithology.

Made in the USA
Columbia, SC
19 November 2021